Chronicles of the Ancient Future

Chronicles of the Ancient Future

by Richard Hoffman

ARPress
ILLUMINATING IDEAS,
EMPOWERING VOICES

ARPress
45 Dan Road Suite 5
Canton MA 02021
Hotline: 1(888) 821-0229
Fax: 1(508) 545-7580

Ordering Information:
Quantity sales. Special discounts are available on quantity purchases by corporations, associations, and others. For details, contact the publisher at the address above.

Printed in the United States of America.

ISBN-13:   Softcover   979-8-89330-062-8
                 Hardcover   979-8-89330-063-5
                 eBook   979-8-89330-064-2

Library of Congress Control Number: 2024901422

FORWARD

Science Fiction has always been fascinated with time travel. It presents many questions that defy answers. One of its primary paradoxes is the ability to change the past.

Example: If a person were to go back into the past and kills his parents, what would be the outcome? The initial answer would be that he would cease to exist, because he would never have been born. However, if he were not born, how could he have killed his parents?

Does this stop us? No, not even close. Then the idea arises that maybe he could not do so because time itself would prevent him from killing his parents. Perhaps traveling through time is some kind of projection into a past that we could not interact with, because we have no form for any kind of interaction.

Another possibility is that we can interact with the past all that we want. However, our interactions in the past would only promote the very objective that we were trying to prevent.

People wrestle with the idea of a predestined future versus a fluid future determined purely by our choices. The latter prevails in our present culture. But is it absolute?

Another assumption made by writers of science fiction is that only large companies, governments, or scientists have created and control over the time machine. Their use of time travel was at their disposal, which was not always good. The relationship between time and life has never been clearly defined.

These explorations present another view of time and planetary life and their purpose.

Table Of Contents

Chapter 0

Purple Stones

Strange mists were swirling all around me. It was as if I was in the middle of some kind of swirling clouds of color. As the mist was dissipating, I could observe shadows of images before me. Very little of the images around me looked familiar. It appeared like that of being inside of some spaceship. I found myself looking at a frontal screen viewing the journey. It was a very huge screen; it made me feel as if I was standing in front of a large window panel that covered the entire wall. I could see the earth coming into view. I heard a voice speaking, but I could not make out the words. It wasn't English words.

Oddly enough, there was a man, a woman and a cat sitting at their consoles looking at their screens. They looked like something straight out of science fiction movie. Their clothing was especially futuristic. Even the cat had a glowing crystal just above from being between its eyes. The cat turned its head and was watching me intently. Then the man noticed the cat looking at me. He said, "Oh, he is here!" in English. The woman then turned to one of the many consoles and flipped a switch. She said, "We should be able to see him now."

He said "Don't be afraid. Our intentions are peaceful. You don't know us, but we know you. We brought you here. Eventually, we will be in contact with your kind in person. But not in the way you might think." She spoke to this being saying that they were on our final approach. I looked at the screen, I saw the Earth enveloping the entire screen. I noticed that North and South America were facing us. Their trajectory was moving us toward North America. As the size of North America grew in size on the screen, I noticed them zooming in on the Mississippi River. The image seemed to focus on the river at the location in which Iowa, Missouri and Illinois existed. We veered westward a little; and I saw Des Moines. This got my attention. As I was contemplating their possible intent, I saw my office building. Then the focus of the view was on the approximate level that my office existed. She said, "Remember the name, Gomez Emmanuel."

Startled by the sight and message, I woke up. It was just a dream! However, it seemed so real, and I forgot to ask them their names. I could not get back to sleep. It was two in the morning. I got out of bed because I did not want to wake up Margo. She was sound asleep. I put the news on the screen in the living room at a low volume. The images in my mind overshadowed the voices and images on the screen. Finally, it was time for her to get up. I couldn't wait any longer to tell her of my dream. I went into the bedroom. I told her about the dream. She told me that it was just a dream. "Don't worry about it. You watch too many science fiction movies. One of them came back and haunted you in your dream."

Overwhelmed by the eerie feeling that dream had left in my psyche; I felt that today was not going to be a normal day. I cut my mid-afternoon snack short at the deli on the first floor of the office building. It was an ominous feeling that I did not understand. How could that dream seem so real? I would have taken the stairs to avoid the elevator, but my office was on the 77th floor. Everything seemed normal when I examined my surroundings. I had this strange feeling that I was being watched. Maybe, it's just being in a new working place. We moved into the new office building last week. At least this was Des Moines, Iowa and not New York City. I did not have to worry about its rioting people, which occurred nearly every day. At least, I did not have to contend with any of them just to get to work this morning. I don't think that I could have handled that today. My nerves were already shot.

The interior of the building was very futuristic looking. My office also had that a similar look to it. After getting inside my office, I looked out the window over the city. The view was awesome; it almost made me forget about the dream. The sun, however, was lowering toward the horizon. One of the neat features about this building was its transition windows. The tint would increase as the sunlight became more direct and intense. Surprisingly, the tinting process was much quicker than my glasses. I also liked the ability to tell the room to turn on or off the lights, lock or unlock the door.

Another great feature was that my wife had an office joined to mine. Although, her job did not require her to be there every day; she could come and work here if her job did not require her to be gone. Today she was judging a case concerning fraud in the financial matter of one of the major farms in Iowa. My job, on the other hand, required me to be here. If someone came to look for me, I had to be here for them. It is just good business. Most of my business, however, could be done over the phone.

Perhaps, this ominous feeling was just some kind projection from my past experiences. It was quiet in the office. My secretary was telling me that there were no phone calls and no scheduled appointments for today. Having no appointments was different. Although this was a rare occurrence, it was needed today to give me time to recover from the dream. So, I decided just to relax and enjoy the view. This was Friday, and it was a long week. Moving into this new office took quite a bit of energy. Then another feeling of urgency came over me. I usually get one of these kinds of feelings when something is about to happen within one of my business ventures.

Paradigm shifts were common to me. Owning a conglomerate of businesses made it inevitable. However, this time, we had two of them over concerning one event. We wanted ever so much to observe the solar eclipse on September 23, 2090. Unfortunate for us, the total eclipse could only be seen off the western coast of Greenland and the southern coasts of Ireland and England or the northern coast of France. We bought tickets last August to travel to London,

England to view it. We were going to make a week visit there. Just two hours before we were to leave the house, I got a call from our office in Florida. The CEO of the company was going to fire 150 of the 170 employees. That is highly irregular. I tried to ascertain the situation over the phone. I was not being lazy; I just did not want to make the trip down there. However, the phone call was of no avail. There were far too many conflicting reports on the quandary. This company was my most recent acquisition; the potential of this newly acquired company was very great. However, this company has become my worst nightmare. So, I went down to resolve the dispute. It was very unpleasant. But it needed to be resolved at the expense of a lovely time with my wife waiting for the eclipse. She was disappointed also. We got our tickets refunded. The money on the specialized glasses was a loss. Comparatively a small loss, but it became a reminder of the loss time we could have had together.

That weekend became important; it was a time for me to relax from my job and get reacquainted with my wife and prepare for watching the solar eclipse. However, it was this Friday at 3:47 PM, September 22, 2090, my plans were about to be interrupted again. I remember that time because I was staring at the clock thinking for just thirteen more minutes and I could leave with a clear conscience. I was anticipating preparing and going out on a picnic tomorrow. We were also going to fake watching the solar eclipse outside. After the incident in Florida, I doubled down on my effort to see the eclipse with my wife. Fortunately for me, I was able to be back from Florida in time. I was hoping to leave at an earlier time today, when my secretary informed me, I had a visitor. The message was that he needed to see me about an important matter. Reluctantly, I decided to see this individual. He asked, "Is this Richard Hoffman Inc." I replied that it was, and that I am the owner. Then I asked him not to think of me as rude in not seeing you today. It is because I wanted to view the solar eclipse with my wife tomorrow. Afterwards, I would investigate his proposition. He agreed to meet me on Monday at 8:00 in the morning on September 25, 2090. I told him to leave his name and appointment date with my secretary on the way out. Again, I forgot to ask for his name. Just like in my dream. As I was ready to leave to go home, I received a phone call about some paperwork that the building manager needed. After filling out the paperwork, I rushed home.

Even though we could not go to England to observe this phenomenon, we still had our alternate plan to observe the eclipse. Prior to the picnic and the eclipse, we took our large screen out to a park and hooked it up to our phone and connected ourselves with a cable station to view the eclipse. Yes, it was a crazy thing to do, but I wanted to make it as special as I could. The eclipse was spectacular. The best pictures came near sunrise in France. We were watching the cable's scheduled west coast showing. Others around us asked to look on with us. By the time the eclipse was over, we had about thirty people joining us. Afterward, we had a good picnic. The food was absolutely scrumptious, and I loved the time reconnecting with my wife. The weather was a little cool, but it was enjoyable. After getting back home and helping my wife to put our house in order, I puzzled over the nature of my future appointment, and what it might entail.

Keeping this scheduled appointment, I met with the owner of a mining company, Gomez Emmanuel. The dream came back to me. This was the name I heard in the dream! I must not relate this information; otherwise, he may think there is something wrong with me. Then I continued listening to his conversation.

He said that their kids were visiting some relatives. While they were there visiting outside of Lima, their kids were playing in an empty countryside field across from their aunt. They found some shiny purple crystalline rocks. These rocks were heavier than normal rocks. Contrarily to our original thought, the purple color was superficial to the substance. He opened a mining operation that was in Peru outside of Lima by about 20 miles northwest. These stones that the kids found were composed of uranium that was not radioactive. These unique rocks were apparently found only in that location. They were setting up the site to mine this rare form of uranium. Then I interrupted his presentation and interjected some pertinent questions. For one, how did they know that it was uranium for it was not radioactive? Did he have any samples of it? He was patient with me and answered my questions. He said that after they purified it, it had a specific gravity of 18.22. If it were iron, its specific gravity would be 7.86, and lead has a specific gravity of 11.34.

Uranium, however, has a specific gravity of 19.05. Therefore, he thought it must be some other element or compound. Further examination, by him, of this material showed that it was indeed uranium. The substance had 92 electrons; therefore, it had only 92 protons. The difference was in the number of neutrons. In the known radioactive uranium, the neutrons outnumber the protons by 54 nucleons. The atomic structure of this substance had considerably less neutrons. In this sample, the number of neutrons equals the number of protons giving 184 nucleons. This kind of relationship between protons and neutrons in large nuclei is highly improbable. The substance must have been manmade or perhaps even alien made. Probably, it is the latter because we do not have the technology to produce such a substance. Alien-made stuck with me in view of the dream.

Even though the scientific notation of this substance is Uranium-184, he called the non-radioactive substance "cold uranium." I liked the sounds of the term; it may have some marketing value. I asked him of the uses for this cold uranium. He was not sure of any, but it would be considered a novelty mineral or isotope. I also asked him if the cold uranium could become radioactive. His reply was- "absolutely not." Cold uranium maintains a purely crystalline structure alternating the protons and neutrons within its nucleon structure in all dimensional directions." He had with him a report made from the subatomic analysis of the substance. He handed it over to me to read.

Reading the subatomic analysis of the substance was equally fascinating. It explained in detail the reason that this form of uranium was non-radioactive. It also gave an overview about radiation stating that the radiation of a substance occurs at the nucleus of an atom. This phenomenon occurs when two neutrons encounter each other or if there is a lone neutron. The entire purpose of the radioactive process was to transform a neutron into a proton. In uranium and other elements, the process occurs because one or more neutrons are touching. Within his sample of uranium, there are no extra neutrons to cause such a phenomenon. There was only one way this isotope of uranium would ever become radioactive. This could only be accomplished by interjecting neutrons onto the surface of the nucleus. These neutrons will encounter one of the neutrons of the original nucleus or with one of the other added neutrons. Without doing this, this atomic nucleus is very stable. This is true for any nonradioactive element.

Three samples were given to me. One was of iron, the second was lead, and the other was this material that he claimed to be non-radioactive uranium. They all had the same volume, but the iron sample was the lightest. The cold uranium has the heaviest of the three, about two and a half times as heavy as iron. He said that this substance formed a single vein leading us some distance under the ground. They had equipment that was shipped to them to examine the scope of the vein. The equipment was old and could not ascertain the actual depth of the vein. They made an unofficial projection that it may reach beyond 500 feet. Without better equipment, he could not say for certain anything of the true nature of the vein.

He told me that he spent two months seeking someone to invest in his project. All the local businesses in Peru were strapped for money and could not help him. A friend of his heard that I was into investing in such undertakings. He showed me all his documents concerning the finding. His expedition intrigued me. Cold uranium is unnatural. If it were artificially produced, how could a manmade substance be in a mineral vein? Why in Peru? Yet, the data was before me; this could really be a money maker.

Possibilities were limitless. We could make numerous trinkets of this material. They would have to be small because of the weight. This mineral is so rare that people will be willing to pay exorbitant prices just for the novelty of owning such a substance. Thoughts of these possibilities staggered my mind. Soon I forgot about whether the substance was being manmade or being alien-made, or even why anyone would ever create such a substance.

Remembering the dream, he thought more about the possibility of being alien-made. Wondering to himself, "Is this what the dream was about? It couldn't be. What interest would aliens have in me making an extra buck? Perhaps the dream was some kind of prelude to some other purpose. It does seem to have the possibility of making me extremely rich. In any case, I need to explore this avenue more, or at least until I get some answers."

Signing the paperwork necessary for the project was more tedious than I expected. Afterwards, I went home. I talked to my wife about taking a trip to Peru. She wanted to come along because she had never been to South America. After making some arrangements, we joined Gomez in Lima. It was a pleasant flight down to Peru. We had only two short layovers. We were excited to be down there and took a little tour of the city of Lima.

Gomez had a beautiful house facing the Pacific Ocean. We met his wife and children. He introduced me to Ocho, who found the two stones. I asked him about his discovery. He told me that he was playing baseball with his relatives just before dinner. The position assigned to him was the one that a ball's arrival rarely occurs being far from the batter. Just before dinner, a ball connected with the swing of the bat. The ball went high and long. It flew over his head. He chased the ball for some distance. The ball had already stopped rolling by the time he got to it.

As he was running toward the ball, he saw a lady throw something onto the ground near the ball and walk away. As he went to pick up the ball, he saw something twinkle. On the ground near the ball were two metallic purple stones crystalline in nature. They were beautiful to look at. He wondered why the lady would throw them away. He picked them up and they were heavy. Yet, she tossed them as wadded paper. Perhaps the stones were not thrown by her, but by something else. After picking them up, he looked for that lady and did not see her. Then he noticed by the location of the stones was the same material embedded in the ground.

At any rate, the other kids were calling for him to hurry up as supper was ready. The rockhound side of him surfaced and he could not throw the stones back to the ground. After all, they were unusual. He rushed as much as he could with the stones in his pockets. He did not want the stones to tear his pockets. He could hardly wait to tell his dad.

I thought it was interesting that a lady would possibly throw these stones away. Perhaps, she was a hiker, and the stones were too heavy to carry. He said they never saw that lady again after that day. Still, there was something nagging in the back of my mind, wondering what role this lady has with the stones.

Gomez said that they searched for the lady. They called the police for assistance in finding this lady. They put ads in the newspaper, radio, and cable networks. There was no one that responded with any validity. Some were looking for money; others were looking for some kind of notoriety. After two months we felt confident about continuing our project. One other item to consider was that even if she threw the stones to the ground, how would she know that there would be a vein of the same material at that same location?

Dinner was great. Ocho was a character. He was really excited about those stones. True, they were unique. The impression he gave was that he found the Holy Grail of stones. Perhaps, he did. We made plans to visit the site tomorrow. The night went by fast as we were exhausted from our day. At breakfast, we did not eat much because of the excitement over the discovery. We saw the kids off to school. Afterward, we left Lima to examine the location.

Looking at the site, I observed nothing especially impressive about the location. The crew did some more digging around the site looking for more possible veins of the substance. There was none on the surface. However, the site did have a relatively large and thick metallic purple jagged line. This was obviously the top of some kind of vein. Certainly, this vein could go down 500 feet. However, I am just an amateur. So, they did some underground mapping to examine the area for the extent of the cold uranium deposit. The report showed that this particular vein went down 1,000 feet. However, while they were mapping, they found 2,000 feet underground that there was a cavern that was lined with cold uranium. This deposit was not seen previously because of the poor quality of the previous equipment. At first, they thought it was some kind of instrument echo. They took the equipment to other locations only to find the same information. Astonishing also was that the cavern was not a typical cavern. It was a perfect cube measuring 750 feet per dimensional direction. The cavern must be manmade. That which started out to be a mining project became an archeological expedition.

Another observation was that there were objects on the floor of the cube. Among the objects sensed were three large objects forming a row on the eastern side of the cube. Moreover, they could not find any corridor leading into the cube. Gomez was quick in putting together another project upon finding the cube. He was very excited about the finding and thought that I would be interested in the project. His pitch was honest, saying that while it could be expensive, it might be the greatest archeological find in history. The idea excited me. But I kept a straight face. I agreed to fund this expensive expedition with the stipulations that I was to be one of the first people into the embedded cube and to co-lead the expedition.

Afterwards, I thought about the conditions that I set. They were a little overbearing. I communicated my misgivings to my wife. She had me talking to Gomez about it. He understood my excitement about all the prospects of the endeavor. He thought that he might have done the same thing if the circumstances were different. I told him that I really did not need to co-lead the expedition. Gomez said that perhaps it would be best if I did, having experience in running a multi-business company. His only request was that he be given credit for the discovery. I agreed, at least that.

We worked on the paperwork and submitted it to the Peruvian government. This took a little time for them to process it. We took some time for a little tourism. We visited some of the ancient Inca ruins. They were impressive. One of the sights was Moras Moray. It reminded me of some of the ore mines in the west, except this looked more purposeful. Then we saw the ancient runways and images that could only be seen from the air. It was quite spectacular. The papers were finally approved. Our next task to accomplish was the coordination with the different contractors. This took a little time as well. Finally, we had everybody ready to go to the site. After arriving, we still had to organize our efforts among the different contractors. We decided to do the mining and archeology dig simultaneously. Our focus was primary on the cube than on the uranium. Even so, the mining project became very lucrative.

There was a little snag with bringing the drilling equipment to the site. The traffic was a problem in Lima. Eventually, we had to improvise a route to the location. That was an unexpected expense for the project. However, we were still well within our budget. Finally, the equipment had to be inspected for damage during transport. Finally, the interlude with civil engineers came to an end.

Chapter 1

The Machine

Schools in Lima were having a break for a teacher conference. Their kids were home with us that day. So, we took them with us to the site. During the groundbreaking ceremony, their kids were playing at a respectful distance from the workplace. Excitement welled up within me as the drills finally started drilling into the earth. It felt good. I was embarking on some incredible find. We brought a picnic lunch with us. Margo and I celebrated with George and his family. We prayed for good success and ate our food watching the drill working its way into the ground.

When the drill reached the chamber, a blast of air spewed out of the hole for a few seconds. Apparently, the cube was pressurized for some unknown reason to us. Then we pulled out the drill leaving a hole with a diameter of five inches. There was this eerie sky-blue glow at the base of the hole. Before we made the hole wide enough for human beings to journey down into the embedded cube, we sent down a camera.

Images from the camera were equally bewildering. Instead of rough rock faces, the walls, ceiling and floor were smooth. Their coloring appeared to be a dim glowing sky-blue. Just as the GPR (Ground Penetrating Radar) equipment indicated, there were objects on the floor. However, they were not in disarray, everything was in excellent condition. The only debris that we found was from our drilling into the cube. Otherwise, there was not even a discernable trace of dust to be found of any kind.

Some months later, we completed a shaft big enough to send down people. Afterward, we had to install an elevator. The elevator was also a hard achievement; we wanted it to be as unobtrusive as possible. We couldn't wait for the elevator. We decided to visit the cube before the construction of the elevator. We made a good-sized basket. We attached it to a couple of cables and had the construction workers use a crane to let us down. I, of course, wanted to be one of the first people to explore this structure and examine its contents. After we descended into the chamber, we first examined the walls of the chamber. They were indeed smooth, not rock, but it had a glassy mirror like appearance. When we shined our flashlights upon it, the regions of impact by the lights produced from our flashlights turned from sky-blue to white. The cold uranium lining of this room was beyond the interior surface of the room. The cold uranium was about two inches thick. The sky-blue mirror was about a half inch thick. Evidently, from that which we could ascertain, it was used to strengthen the walls, making it more solid than the surrounding mantle of the earth.

In the exact middle of the room was a nine-foot pillar about one foot and a half in diameter, and white in color. Above this pillar was a large crystal sphere. It was floating only about a couple of inches above it. The diameter of the sphere is about twelve feet. No light was radiating from the sphere. Seven recliners, also white, were evenly spaced from the eighth location. The arrangement of these seven recliners was radial in nature from the pillar, forming a wedge having a span of exactly 45 degrees apart around the pillar. Each recliner existed 60 feet away from the pillar. Their centerlines intersected at the center of the pillar exactly. These recliners were in a bed-like position. Each recliner had the capability to pivot in place.

Archways existed another nine feet beyond the recliners in the same radial manner. Each archway measured on the inside twenty-seven feet tall and twelve feet wide. The thickness of the archway sides was four and a half feet square at the base, and it seemed uniform throughout the structure. They were also white in color; both the arches and pillar surfaces were like fine sandpaper. On the outer left side of the archway, there was a shelf attached without a seam. It measured one and a half foot by one and a half foot, and it was four and a half feet above the floor. This shelf had a small ridge around its edge. There is an indentation in the archway next to the shelf about an inch away, facing the pillar. There was no door in the archway. Upon the shelf, there was a helmet. Under the helmet, in the middle of the shelf a nine-inch square and two inches deep, was a compartment for a medallion filled with crystals.

Behind the pillar at the eighth location was a podium-like structure. Its base was about twelve feet square and elevated by four and a half feet. Nine steps led up to from either side. There was a futuristic chair and a terminal of some kind in front of it. These were aligned facing west. Behind the podium were three immense obelisks uniform in size. We estimate that each was 675 feet tall and 48 feet by 96 feet at the base. The widest dimensions of the obelisks were facing the wall about 45 feet away from the eastern wall.

There were no wires found to connect these devices, I suppose that they could have been buried under the floor. We examined the podium more thoroughly and found that under the monitor screen was a control panel. Under the podium table was a storage place for eight crystals. There was also a helmet for the person at this location. Lastly, perhaps more importantly, there were two books found in this storage cabinet. The pages of the book resembled thin flexible metallic paper, almost like iridescent aluminum foil. One book was thinner than the other by half. The thinner book appears to be a manual. The thicker book seems to be a log. I could almost imagine that it had bolded dates and indented entries in its log. However, the written characters were undecipherable even though it was neatly typed.

Controls upon the control board or consol were also peculiar. On the right side of the consol was a lever with a handling grip on top. This lever could slide away or toward the operator at the consol. The range of this lever was about one foot and a half. Near the top of its sliding range about one inch from the top was a notch going to the right. However, the position of the lever was about 6/7ths of the way down from the top. I moved the lever away from its original position, nothing happened. I released the lever, and it returned to its original position. I even tried moving the lever to the notch. There was still no response; it still returned to its original position when I released it. I was hoping for some kind of response. Perhaps, it was fortunate that there was no response. We were being a little reckless; we had no inkling of an idea of the function of the machine. For all we knew, it could be some elaborate planet destroyer. However, in all likelihood, that would not be the function of the machine.

Another feature the consol had, going left from the lever, was a row of eight crystals, a line of seven and one slightly separated from the seven, protruding from the surface of the control panel. As for the coloring of the crystals, each was clear as glass. Under each crystal was a vertical row of five buttons. The top button on each row was green, the bottom button was red, and all the others were blue. Below the columns of buttons was a keyboard. The letters on the keyboard were the same character set found in the books. The only keys we recognized were the arrow keys.

On the far left-hand side of the control board was another lever. Unlike the other lever, it pivoted in one location. Originally this lever was in a vertical position, or that was the way we found it. When we moved this lever, it remained in the position in which we moved it. We stationed the lever back into the position where we found it.

There were three switches at the bottom of the control panel. They only had on and off positions. Again, there was no response from flipping them, so we returned them to the position in which we found them. That seems to be the extent of the control panel. Above the control panel was a monitor having approximately 72 inches in measurement diagonally across the screen, it was a goodly size for a monitor. It had no image displayed. The control panel rested upon the podium.

Our next task was to examine the obelisks. We found that it has embedded crystals of different colors and sizes. They were not randomly placed; they were in some complex pattern that repeated itself every 54 feet. The total times that it repeated were 12 times with a foot and a half space between each repetition. There was an empty region above and below the crystals about 6 feet on the bottom, and about 27 feet at the top. Each obelisk had the same characteristics. The surface in which the crystals were embedded was smooth and black. When we shined light upon it, no light reflected, at least not any that we could discern. It looked like the crystals were suspended in midst of a void. We knew it was not a void because we could feel the surface. The crystals reflect the light from our sources of light, but nothing beyond that. We brought in some instruments to examine these obelisks; each of the obelisks appeared to be solid as if every cubic inch were being utilized for some function.

As stated earlier, the only mess we found was from drilling into the place, which we promptly cleaned up. There was no other dust in this place! The atmospheric content was near that of the surface. The oxygen content was a little higher, and the nitrogen was a little lower. Naturally, there was the usual trace of argon. We returned to the surface bewildered about our discovery. Obviously, our discovery had great archeological value. However, looking at the find as a collection of artifacts was not satisfying; It did not seem right to bring up these items to sell these items. These items had a purpose, and I wanted to know what the purpose of these objects was. Moreover, I needed to know how to make this mechanism worked.

Questions kept running through my mind. Who built this cube with its machines? Where did they come from? How did they get into the room? How do they refresh the air in the room? More to the point: What was the function of this room? Why did they embed it? What caused the mechanism to be abandoned? None of us that went down into the embedded room were able to comfort our minds over these issues. As Margo and I were pondering these things, Gomez came knocking at our door.

Gomez told me that there was something familiar about the characteristic of the measurements. They were not using the metric system; their measurements don't come out to even meters or centimeters. Their measurements do not use the English measurements. However, there was a common ancient measurement. That is a cubit.

When he went over the data about the measurements and converted them into cubits. There were no fractions; they became exact cubit measurements. The dimension of the cube measured exactly to 500 cubits. The dimension of each obelisk becomes 450 by 64 by 32 cubits. The interior measurement of each archway becomes 18 by 8 cubits. The structural base of the archway's sides becomes three by three. The central pillar: six cubits by one cubit by one cubit. The sphere has a diameter of eight cubits. The list goes on. In each instant the measurement is a whole number of cubits! Perhaps, this is just a coincidence. Does it mean that this device was made by our ancestors? Why would we return to measuring in cubits in the future? Perhaps the aliens taught mankind to measure by cubits. At any rate, he thought it as being peculiar. I didn't let that bother me. Whoever built this equipment was extremely advanced in technology; they would not necessarily be limited to whole numbers. Perhaps the books that we uncover will illuminate us on this issue.

Journeying back home was somewhat slow because of my desire to find answers. After getting back to Des Moines, Iowa, I went to the University of Iowa in Iowa City about 112 miles east of my office. Examination of the two books proved difficult, the metallic-like paper contained undecipherable characters. Some of the recognizable characters resembled well formed pre-Babylonian ancient Hebrew. Even after examining the illustrations showing operational procedures, I could not ascertain any purpose for following them. For eight months, the university tried to decipher the manual without availing anything. If it was an alien language, we might not be able to decipher it at all.

Wiping some of the cobwebs out of his brain, Gomez recalled some of his archeological past. He gave me a call. He told me that he was into archeology in his youth, but he went into mining because it was profitable. It occurred to Gomez that the resemblance to Hebrew by some of the characters was a hint. Moreover, the lack of spacing between words within a given line is also indicative of the nature of ancient Hebrew text. I relayed that information to the university. In fact, it was by using the Hebrew language that they discovered that the thinner book was indeed a manual to a time machine.

Written in the appendix of the manual was their formulation of cold uranium that we found. They combined 46 nuclei of helium-4 to make a single cold uranium nucleus. To achieve this product, they had the conversion machine in a room near absolute zero to slow the isobaric spin of the helium nuclei. Using electromagnetic energy, they pulled the electrons away from the nucleus. The pattern in which these nuclei exist was depicted as a square divided into fourths forming four smaller squares. They then colored two of the squares opposite diagonally from each other black the remaining two white. White represented the protons and black for the neutrons.

Combining these helium nuclei was a fascinating process. They made five larger square plates or 'flakes' as they called it. Each of these plates contains nine helium nuclei. Each of the helium squares was facing the same way per plate. The resulting image as shown in their diagram was a square divided into sixths on both dimensional axes resulting in 36 nucleons. The second plate was the inverse of the previous one, alternating back and forth their patterns. For the inverse pattern, they just flipped the plate. Each plate had 18 protons. Since five times 18 equals 90, the final helium nucleus was bonded to the center of the top flake keeping with the alternating pattern between protons and neutrons. In this, cold uranium was created. Now we know, the builders of the machine made the substance… but who were they? I am also wondering: How long did it take them to make the amount of cold uranium needed for the cube?

The second larger book was indeed a log. In the log, there were accounts of the machine being used for historical fact finding, scientific studies, judicial purposes, psychology, and other minor purposes. There were some blank pages at the end of the log. They could have had even more journeys. Why did they stop? Why, if they did, abandon the project? Perhaps, some catastrophe occurred.

Analyzing the text in front of the log, we found that the machine operated under the influence of some ethereal record of time. It was able to recall data from each instant in history both in the past and the future as if it were all prerecorded. One entry in the log was about some of the attempts to change history. These attempts failed miserably. In fact, their attempts to change history was needed to fulfill the actual historical accounts. Yet other attempts came to naught from failure to accomplish the required task. Inversely, when they tried to alter the future, their very act caused it to happen. Yet, there were some things in the future that could be changed. However, the result of the change did not change the overall direction of events. It is as if we were given free will to choose, but the choices that we make are already known and recorded. Example, the building and usage of this machine was also recorded. Responses to the data received from the machine were also part of the recorded record.

Example: One account of its usage was to solve a murder. Though there was much deception concerning the case. They were able to go back in time and solve the case, and the machine had already had the influence of machine incorporated within the whole scenario recorded!

At first, I thought the three obelisks were storage devices of time data. But they were used to access recorded time. Each obelisk had to be synchronized just to access the ethereal record of time. By the time we acquired the machine, they had already worked out the bugs in the system. These changes were already incorporated into the logic board. Then they could access the time lever to pinpoint the time selected by the user. The top of the obelisks represented the end of the future, and the base was the beginning of time. All of this was accessed by the magnified brainwaves produced by the crystals.

Examination of the manual also revealed that there were living quarters available to them under the cube. This was accessed by pressing against an indentation behind the console platform. We found the indentation and pressed it. The podium slid forward. There was a stairway leading to a large room underneath. On the two opposing sides were four evenly spaced doors that could slide open. Each was an entrance to a bedroom; each had a private bathroom. There was an entrance to a room behind the main room. This room was more like a dining room. Kitchen appliances were embedded in its surrounding walls. In the main room, there was an indentation by the entrance from the cube. We pressed it, and a large table rose up from the floor and eight well designed chairs unfolded from the floor. Lights came from the edges formed between the walls and the ceiling. We felt like we stepped into some kind of futuristic facility. The doors could be opened both by command and by manually pushing the buttons. However, the commands were not in English; we used the buttons.

Dealing with the public during this time was an issue. We were still very secretive about the cube. We wanted to know if the cube worked before making any news report. None of us wanted 'egg on our faces.' We needed eight people to be within our expedition team that would be willing to try to operate the machine, myself included in the count. We were extremely excited about having the translated manual. We were eager to get back down to Peru to operate the embedded cube. We followed each step carefully. We had each person place their crystal in the helmet which they were to use in sequence. We positioned the recliners to face the pillar. We were all staring into the crystal sphere to turn the machine on. In essence, the result would be to ignite the spherical crystal. Since I was at the podium, I was the last to insert the crystal into the helmet and donned it. I pushed all the green buttons under their respective crystals. Then I put my hand on the time lever.

Nothing happened! After deciphering the manual, we were still not able to operate the device. Did we mistranslate the manual? Was the machine broken? We did not know. All we were able to accomplish was a little static on the monitor. That gave us a clue- It operated on brainwaves that we were barely able to produce. My objection to this conclusion was that these crystals placed in our helmets were supposed to amplify our brainwaves. However, the brainwaves that we were emitting into the crystal were weaker than that the crystal demanded. We were able to simulate these stronger brainwaves by using electromagnetic energy. We amplified our brainwaves until the crystal responded. The initial response was that the crystal glowed as a dim red light. That was still not enough.

Our quest then became finding people that could generate such brainwaves. We spent several months searching for such individuals. We tried university students, professors, or anyone that we thought to be very smart. We even tried those who thought to have extra sensory perception. When we hooked them up to the crystal, it was still nearly void of activity. Then we turned to athletic people, whose bodies were in very good shape. Again, that was a failure. The quest was squelched harshly. There was not a person with such brain power, leave alone finding eight such people.

Technology came to the rescue. We were able to use another method to amplify and transform our brainwaves into a pattern acceptable to the crystals. Fortunately for us, these devices did not interfere with the helmets. The beautiful aspect of this technology was anyone hooked up to these devices could access the crystals. This gave us breathing room in selecting the people that were to be in the research expedition. Having the ability to access the crystal was no longer a factor. We now could choose for ourselves experts in any given field.

Looking further into the manual, it answered some of my questions that were troubling me. My primary concern was maintaining the oxygen content of the room. Although we could not see it, there was a large teleporting device in front of the room which displaced the air from the room with air from a location high in the troposphere. A person does not want to be standing in that part of the cube's floor when the mechanism is operating. It would teleport anything within that space into the atmosphere. From there, they will fall over twenty thousand feet or more.

Moreover, the builders also built a small room upon the surface to teleport people into the embedded room. Teleportation is probably the wrong word. The writers were speaking of an ability of strengthening brainwaves by using a special crystal formula. A person could phase into another location by using a crystal to harness the intent of the brainwave. From the description within the manual this device was in a room 17 degrees westward from being directly above the time machine. It must have been destroyed long ago. We cannot find any kind of structure, foundation or anything indicating that there was ever such a structure on the surface above the uranium cube.

Ashamed of ourselves for keeping this project secret for as long as we did, we decided it was time to present our find to some degree. The locals in Peru were beginning to be asking questions, and I did not want to lie to them. Therefore, a statement went out to the press for two reasons. One, we wanted to inform the public of our find. Two, we were looking for people experts in certain fields to go on our expeditions. The article explained to them that these expeditions would be very time-consuming. Secondly, the 'equipment' may have ceased to function properly.

The selection of people to utilize this machine went through much controversy. Some thought only historians should be allowed to use it. Others thought only scientists could appreciate what the machine offered. Yet others saw it as a tool to be used only for legal purposes. Some even suggested that it be reserved for religious endeavors. Others saw it as a tool for the military. After the free-for-all, we decided to send two historians, two scientists, two religious' scholars, one judge and myself. It was agreed that I would be the one operating the machine. There was too much opposition to sending anyone from the military, so we decided against doing that.

Extremists were already making an overly excessive uproar over using the machine. People came out of the woodwork opposing any usage of the machine. Most of them were paranoid that we would destroy the very fabric of time. None of which, they could prove. We had the alien manual to help us to settle their conundrum of arguments. aside. Then, it was a matter of finding experts to fill those positions.

Gomez did not want to go because the expeditions would take him away from his family for long periods of time. He had a couple of preschool children that he wanted to be involved in their development. My wife and I would have felt the same way if we had children. Speaking of my wife, she has judicial experience. She is a very good one. It would be nice for her to come along. I must go; my money is tied up in this project.

We decided to look in America for our companions because of the need to be able to communicate readily in real time. Fortunately for us, the journey home was relaxing. We had much to accomplish.

We made ads for the newspapers, radio programs and cable networks about our project. It wasn't for the state of Iowa, but for every state. We also made pitches at the universities. It truly was an exhaustive effort.

Overwhelmed by the responses from the articles, I had to leave my office. My office was swamped with resumes. A good majority of them looked pretty good, but I had to narrow it down to six. Not seven, because my wife decided to go with me. My wife suggested that I did not have to narrow it down by resumes alone, throw a banquet. We set the date of the banquet a couple of months away to facilitate those who were to come. I could invite the top seven per position for a total of 42. Before the evening was through, I should have a good grasp of who to bring into the expedition. I should be able to narrow the number down to 42. I was sure that some of them were writing in their resumes things they thought that I wanted to hear and not the facts. I know I can weed those individuals out with somewhat ease about it. We sent out the invitations. Margo and I relaxed and went on a short trip to the Mississippi River to refresh our minds before the banquet.

Tonight was the night of the banquet. I was excited and apprehensive as well. Apprehension existed because I could make a mistake in judgment. Three thoughts plagued me. Not only if their credentials were valid, but they could spend the time needed to complete a long expedition. Secondly, my focus was not only for one position but six. These people will need to be able to work together. Lastly, I wondered if the machine would work. Even with our technology involved, it may not be enough, or the machine was broken.

Dressed and ready to host the occasion, we entered the room with all the people. Everyone was friendly. My wife was as beautiful as always. For the most part it was pleasant. My wife and I made sure to meet everyone. It was a little time consuming but necessary. We also watched to see how these people reacted to each other and note their personalities. I was asking them questions about their field to see if they were genuine. There were some of those that I could eliminate immediately. Encounters with some proved difficult. They either had big egos, or there was something that did not quite add up. Yet, there were others that were quite likable. We had decided beforehand that we were going to choose three men and three women. There should be, hopefully, at last three men and three women that qualify.

Finally, we were able to narrow it down to six people. We excused everyone at midnight. We took their nametags as they went out the entrance of the banquet room. We kept the name tags of the ones that we chose. We separated from the rest and told them they would be contacted tomorrow. I felt good about the team that we selected. We went home exhausted, but in good spirits.

Next morning, we assembled our list to the Peruvian Consulate for work visas. For each person, we submitted the required documents. They made a special request for a little information about everyone. Part of the reasoning for the request was that time travel seemed somewhat beyond commonsense. The information given to them was gathered from our banquet held for this occasion. The following is the information that we gathered about our team.

George Simmons has been a scientist for 20 plus years. He is 57 years old. He is a professor at Washington State University teaching physics. Military life also colored his view on life; he spent four years in the service. He used the VA funds to get a start in college. Some people go into the military, and afterwards the experience has little impact upon their lives. This is not the case with him. The self discipline that it taught was important to him. His marksmanship was excellent. He kept the skill alive by going to the shooting range every other week. He enjoys hunting for seasonal food. He feels that it gives him a license to eat meat.

His wife died three years ago in a car accident. After the accident, he became more cynical about life. His religious views put him in a borderline atheist category. Naturally, he is a science fiction buff. He joined the team to help to explore technology of different cultures in time.

Cynthia Flynn is a Botanist. She graduated 5 years ago from Ohio State. She has no family, even though she has one daughter, who is in grade school. Her daughter lives with her father, because of some trickery on his part. It was a messy divorce. However, she has pulled herself out from depression by focusing on science. Through much studying in botany, she has all the different major species of plants memorized. She joined to examine plant 'evolution,' if any.

She too believes the idea of going into different eras of time to be exciting. While going into the past shows the development of the present, the future has a certain mystique about it. She has dreams of a future utopia, where people have learned their lessons that time would have taught them.

Jonathan Briggs is a historian. He has analyzed the different cultures' rise to power and their fall. His observation of humanity is that they do not learn from history. Disappointed in life, he never took a wife. He joined our expedition because he has seen patterns in history that have disturbed him, especially in today's culture in America. He had made some predictions that were generated by his study of the patterns.

He wants to go into the future to see if these patterns continue to progress, or if there is a chance for change. The present condition of the human race really depresses him. It seems that half of the population has turned into zombies believing lies and hating the truth. Moreover, they accuse the truth of being fabricated tales of hate. If this pattern continues, he fears that society is headed for 1984. His nightmare was that the 'Ministry of Truth' would be erected only to publish the propaganda of the state.

Samantha Xavier, a historian herself, has another angle to historical data. She wonders about the accuracy and continuity of the available historical data. She wants to go into the past and verify that the data is true. She has not married yet. She is beautiful, but she is waiting for that special someone. Despite her cynical view of history and being very beautiful, she has a very pleasant personality. She is not haughty or manipulative.

Primarily, she wants to go into the past and fill in the gaps in recorded history. Most of the history taught in classes has been rewritten history for political reasons. While this is disturbing enough, there are opportunities lost. She believes that if we could understand history for what it was, we would be better equipped to make a better future.

Joseph Goldberg is a Rabbi. He is the oldest member of the team, being 67 years old. His wife passed away seven years ago because of old age. He was also very excited to undertake this expedition. He wanted an opportunity to experience biblical data as it occurred. He especially desired to witness the life of Moses, Moshe as he called him. He would also like to talk to Noah (Noach in his language). But there were other figures in scriptures that he wanted to see as well. On the other side of the coin, he wanted to go into the future. He wanted to see the way the future unfolds into that which was foretold by Scriptures.

Ruth Bernstein was somewhat hesitant about going on such an expedition. She thought that this was another attempt to discredit the scriptures. But curiosity overcame the doubtful prospects of the adventure. Historical data that this machine could provide might prove quite valuable to her. She is married to a career officer in the army. They don't have any kids. They thought that they might adopt one later next year. He does black ops missions and spends years away from home.

Her primary interest was the relationship of a particular culture has with God. She notes that the present culture is drifting away. She wondered to what magnitude this drift would be allowed to continue before repercussions occur without recourse. She believes she has witnessed some of it already. Furthermore, she believes that these repercussions have not yet reached their crescendo.

Margo Hoffmann, being a judge in the court system of Florida, saw the possibility that the machine could be used to uncover hidden information and expose deception in cases involving criminal activity. She was also looking into some older cases, some famous and others not so much. There are many unsolved cases in our history. She met me when I was looking for legal advice when I was dealing with some shady businessmen in acquiring property. She is a very lovable person, even if I do say so myself. We have had our disappointments in scheduling time to be together. For the most part she has kept a positive attitude.

Richard Hoffman- I am a fortunate businessman who was able to seize the opportunity to sponsor and participate in this expedition. I have always been a science fiction fan. This is an opportunity to participate in the greatest scientific discovery ever. I was selected to oversee this mission because I was the least essential to the mission and I paid the expenses that our missions required. Although, I did have knowledge of the Hebrew language somewhat; it was not part of the criteria. On a personal note, I find the honesty and integrity of the team members to be exceptional. That was my primary concern.

Then I gave some extra information about myself. I tried to be forthcoming as possible. Dealing with people all my life, I have seen the pitfalls of being too honest. Being too cagey also had its downfalls. However, I did have a genuine interest in time travel, and was very curious about the machine. It became more about the discoveries than about the money. These could alter the course of human history. Despite my altruistic attitude, I did see many financial opportunities within taking on this adventure.

Returning to the embedded room in Peru was quite an affair. We played it up. The eight of us were given uniforms to wear. They were purple in color; we all had a patch with the image of a sky-blue cube on our right shoulder. They really outdid themselves. We had cameras pointed at us as we descended using the elevator into the room with the time machine.

Interviews were done in the room after everyone had reached the bottom floor in our elevator that we constructed. There were about seven reporter teams that went down with us. Some of the television news stations I never heard of, like QXB. What it stands for... I don't know, don't care. Oh wait! I do remember! It stood for Quanta Extended Broadcast. It wasn't just a station but a method of recording. They sell their recordings to various broadcasting stations.

The government of Peru helped us set up a stage within the room for the interview eight chairs for us and two for the interviewers. We had to present ourselves one by one giving a little background history of our lives and our reason for going on this expedition. We gave them our names and backgrounds. Then the host asked them some group questions.

These questions were to be answered by a show of hands among the team. The first question was "Do you think time travel will benefit our society?" The response was six to two in favor. The next question was "Do you believe that it will clear up any questions?" The response was eight to zero in favor. The last question was "Do you believe that time travel could become a problem? The response for that was two thought it would, one said no, the rest wasn't certain.

After everyone got pictures of the time machine, they set up some recording apparatuses in non-conspicuous locations within the room to record our expedition. After they removed the interviewing stage, they left. We were alone in this eerie room; the light source came from the shiny sky-blue walls and ceiling. It felt like we were outside high above the ground exposed to the elements. It was both beautiful and unsettling. The only thing that seemed out of place was the elevator that we made to access this place.

Chapter 2

Initial Contact

Execution of the access procedure was our next focus. We still were not certain that the machine would work. We brought all the equipment that we thought we could use, including a minicomputer system. We also brought food and personal items for our stay in the cube. According to the manual, there was a need for eight participants to access the machine. It seems that the brainwave energy needed to initiate this device was immense. After being accessed, for some reason it would operate without the helmets. They also had some kind of security protocol involved with the eight users. At any rate, we followed the translated manual to the letter as best as possible.

There was a section in the manual called 'Priming the Machine.' They called it a 'One Time Experience,' whatever that meant. We noted that there was no difference between performing that task and the subsequent usage of the machine. Well, as far as, starting the machine. It was to occur every time different people were using it. But did not relate that there was a different sequence of events to be taken to initiate this priming event. We concluded that we would probably find out the hard way. After all, we knew that we qualified as 'different people.'

Supposedly, there were three levels of time travel. The first level allows us to view the era of time using the ceiling. Within this, the view is like watching a movie screen. There could not be any interactions with those of that era. The second level of travel required us to pass through the archways. Within this level the traveler could walk among the people of the era but could not be seen by them. We could not touch them, nor could they touch or hear us. In essence, we would be like time ghosts. The advantage over time travel level-one is that individual time travelers could travel to different locations outside the group location seen on the ceiling. Level-three time travel puts us into their reality. They can both see and hear and touch us, and we could do likewise. We elected to use the first level for safety reasons, mainly because we did not know what to expect. We did not want to die in the past before we were born or way in the future of our existence.

Selecting a place in time was somewhat of a challenge. Some wanted to go into the future; others wanted to go to the past. I wanted to go to the notch found on the console's time lever slot. I told them it should be a time of some importance; else why put a notch there? Then I told them that there was a possibility that it is as far back into the dinosaur era. That was a mistake. While some were excited about the prospect, others were terrified. One opposition was about the eating habits of a tyrannosaurus. I reminded them that this is a level-one experience. They cannot touch us. Most of them were curious about the purpose of the notch. It was taken to a vote, and the notch won.

Executing the interpreted instructions required us to act in sequence; otherwise, the machine would not activate. That is a security measure. In order to get started, I handed each of them their respective crystal. The sequence was orientated from right to left. Before we could initiate the execution process, we all needed to don the brainwave enhancer, which was like a thin wired cap. The middle position was first, he puts on the helmet sit down on the recliner. Then he puts the crystal, which I gave him, into the indentation just above from being in-between his eyes.

Afterward, the recliner strapped the person into itself with some kind of sensors placement on the face and arms. Then I would push the green button associated to that position. After his process was completed, the next one would follow the same pattern. The sequence given to us was 4, 7, 1, 5, 3, 2 and 6. Because they drew straws of seven different lengths to determine who went to a particular location,

Cynthia went first. It was a terrifying sight to observe them being automatically strapped in and sensors placed on their skin. We were not expecting that response from the recliners. After each of the seven was in place, and their hookup procedures were executed, I put mine on and sat at the console.

Shocked by the sudden movement of the recliners, they grasped the arms of the recliners. Straps tightened over their wrists causing even more panic. The recliners pivoted and elevated quickly to face the central sphere and stopped. We were peering into the sphere involuntarily, or at least, it seemed. I tried to look away but chose not to do so out of curiosity. Staring into the sphere we saw a dim reddish light. It was growing in intensity and changing color. The color change went though the full spectrum of visible light. After reaching violet, the color began to fade into white. The white light was getting very bright. Coupled with all the color changes, there was a hint of swirling clouds. This image engulfed inside the entire sphere. The same image was observed upon the four walls and ceiling forming a 3D hologram. It was impressive.

The audio experience of this process was just as spectacular. The sound started as a low bass rumble and increased in pitch. When the light turned white, the pitch went beyond our hearing. However, the loudness was pressing against our ears. Then we heard a loud explosion. The sound shocked us as we were not expecting its occurrence. Next after that, the straps around their wrists released with the sensors. Then the recliners pivoted and descended back to their original positions. The churning white color turned into a fading mist. The first thing we saw was sky blue. This turned out to be the sky and not the room. Trees appeared, and we saw shadow figures of people and heard faint voices, eventually all the mist cleared.

George spoke up, "I hope that was the 'One Time Experience' that was spoken of within the manual. I would not want to go through that each time."

I replied, "I am with you, on that one. Let's examine what all of that has accomplished."

Disappointed in our view, we found ourselves on the ground just a little above the surroundings. We could hear one of the photographers complain about not being allowed to take more pictures. We did not go anywhere. Then we realized that we were still in the room. Sure enough no one heard us, and we could only walk within the immediate vicinity before hitting a wall. We could still see the objects in the room as semi translucent.

Then I decided to move the pivotal location lever. I moved it slightly to the west. We found ourselves floating over water, specifically the Pacific Ocean. Behind us we could see the coastline of northern South America. Then I moved the lever northward to North America. We followed the roads to Lincoln Nebraska, my hometown. Well, the place where I was born, anyway. I no longer lived there. At any rate, the weather was beautiful. We could hear the traffic and people talking in the downtown area. As I was reminiscing, George asked "Are we going to 'notchland' or what?" I snapped back into reality, and embarrassingly replied "Yes." I pushed the lever to the notch and slid it into the notch.

Colors filled the room and swirled into a white mist. The noises were louder and more disturbing. I heard a crackling like electrical energy. I was thinking there must be some kind of short, but there was no smell of it. Explosions were also occurring. The colored mist faded like the previous mist. Instead of seeing the Lincoln city skyline, we saw unusual-shaped buildings which were very tall. Everything we saw spelled future. We noticed vehicles passing by us. They were not using wheels. They were floating through the air without any apparent propulsion. This is quite the opposite experience than that any of us were expecting. Samantha said, "Where are the dinosaurs?" We were all wondering the same thing.

Voices then could be heard. Since we were at level-one time travel, we knew no one could see, hear, or touch us. This gave us a sense of being safe. The voices became clearer, but we could not understand a word. Why would they be speaking a foreign language? George presented us with a couple of possibilities. One, our country lost a war and foreign people forced their language upon us. Two, the notch is used for the people that built this device to return them to their own home. I went with number two. The next question was "Where is their home?" We even considered that this might be an alien planet because nothing looks familiar. Or perhaps, this is a far future place. Even stranger yet, we could be in the future or past of the alien world. Again, I went with the second option.

Verifying our location proved very difficult since we could not speak their language. The character set of the writing was like that found in the two books that we found within the embedded cube. We took some pictures of the script that we saw on some boxes on a shelf in a mall-like place; these looked different. Perhaps the writing of the boxes was stylized versions of those letters. We also made video and audio recordings of their speech. We also took pictures of the skyline and buildings, just for show and tell. Samantha got a phone call requesting her presence at the university where she was working. It was a reminder we were still on earth in the present time. This was part of being in level-one. We never left our location of being in the cube in Peru. We decided to return home.

Moving the lever out of the notch, the cube went back into swirling colors. I pushed all the red buttons in the inverse pattern of the green buttons as required by the manual. Then I released the time lever. It returned to its original position, and the location lever returned to its vertical position. That surprised me: because when the machine was off, this lever did nothing when it was released. The cube turned back to its sky- blue appearance as the colored mist dissipated. I took the pictures and recordings back to the university which cracked the language coding. We needed a device to translate the language in real time so that we could understand these people. I told the crew that I would contact them when the device was created, and we would set for a time to return to Peru.

Creating the device was not as easy as it might seem. While our society has mechanical language translators that work in real time, this language did not have any sound to letter recognition yet. We hoped that we had enough samples; we took a multitude of them to be analyzed. A few months passed by with no word. I, finally, checked back in with them. They told me that they were still working at it. They had a version that we could test but there were no guarantees.

They said that this version was using Hebrew as its baseline. However, the language spoken there was more complex than expected. There were some very subtle variations in their vowels. Then there were some letters that sound different from those heard in Modern Hebrew.

Excited, I called everyone to go down again to the cube. We decided to use level-two time traveling mode. This will put us into their world; we can do some traveling around without the restrictions of being inside the machine. Feeling safe enough, we were eager to get started. We all gathered in Los Angeles and took a red eye flight to Mexico City. From there we got a regular flight to Lima. Finally, we made it back to the cube. The eerie sky-blue glow presented a welcoming sight to me. Although, it still gave me the sensation that I was not in a room but up some distance into the sky.

Starting the machine up again was somewhat taxing. We were trying to repeat the instructions from the manual to the letter. We even duplicated our position in Lincoln, Nebraska in hopes of returning to the same location in that world. After the colored mist cleared, we saw the same buildings and skyline as we did before. It was beautiful.

Since we were going into the next level of time travel, there were some extra steps required. First, I had to push the middle blue button in each button column. Then the seven took their helmets and placed them on their respective shelves. Each of them then took the crystal off the helmet and placed it in the indentation on the archway next to the shelf. When this was accomplished, the space between the arches turned black. The blackness was not solid. It looked like a void.

Placing their medallions around their necks and pressing their respective central crystals on their medallions. As each pressed the central crystal within their medallion, a black void between the archways cleared showing the same image as the cube. The screen upon the consol turned on. Seven images appeared upon the screen. Under each image there was a panel with green lines that reminded me of vital signs. There was some writing written under them which I could not read. The seven images reflected the view of everyone. My primary function was to monitor the images on the screen.

Constrained? Negative. There was a provision for me to travel with anyone of the seven. According to the manual, the steps that I needed to take were to remove my crystal from my helmet and put my helmet under the desk. Then grab the medallion under the consol and put it around my neck. Place the crystal in the indentation underneath the crystal in the archway. Interestingly enough, these indentations appeared only when the surface was pressed. Otherwise, no one would ever know that they were there. Then I pressed the central crystal within the medallion. The primary function of this secondary procedure was to help anyone who was in trouble. However, on our first time using this level, we were all planning to stick together. Of course, the archway I chose was that my wife was using.

Passing through the archway was an experience. There was a brief sensation of being pulled forward as if we were falling through the archway. After getting on the other side of the archway, the cube seemed to disappear. All that was left was the archway. Although looking through the archway, I could see a partial image of the cube. No one in this period could see the archways except us. For us, we had to commit to memory the location of the archways. None of us wanted to be lost in another time as a ghost. Each must return through the archway in which they came. If we tried to enter another archway, we would just pass through the archway with no transference back to our time.

Gathering information was our next objective. I oversaw the translator. Having only one translator proved awkward. There was a definite need for each of us to have our own device. Still, we were able to gather information. We first tried it out at a park. We were listening in on a mother telling her daughter to let the other children play with the ball. That message came crystal clear. There were no crackling and the translated voice sounded just like hers. We went a little further and heard two students talking about their college classes. One was getting ready to go to class.

Ecstatic about going to college to get real information, we followed her. After some time, we finally made it there. She stopped off at her friend's house and talked about plans for the weekend. This lasted about three minutes. We were worried that she wasn't going to be to class on time. She was not late. She was going to a math class. It was not a high-level course. I thought it would be interesting to see how these people do math. Most of the others thought our time would be better spent elsewhere. Reluctantly, I agreed.

Looking at the buildings around us, we tried to decipher which building would be the administration building. There were many magnificent buildings that held many classrooms. Just by looking through the windows, we could see that the front of the classroom was a single walled viewing station, something like a television. Off to one side was a hologram of a teacher. The chairs that the students sat in folded up and became part of the floor when they left. After doing our scouting of different classrooms, we took the job of finding the administration building more seriously.

Noticing a smaller auditorium building, we walked through the door of it. We saw people sitting behind desks and students standing in line in front of a counter. We were fortunate, they were registering for classes. On a large screen, it showed something like a list of classes and teachers. Hopefully, that list is what we think it is. Joseph took a picture of that and some of the campus maps. Again, we listened in on a conversation of a student at the counter. One student wanted to find a class concerning the history of mining on the moon. I said maybe the translator malfunctioned or maybe not. If the floating vehicles on the road are an indication, this could be a fact.

Deciding that we had enough information, we started back toward the archways. We traveled quite a distance. It took us about an hour to get back. Anxious about getting that screen translated, we did only that was necessary to return home. We took it to my home university to have it examined. The process took a bit of time. They had to convert the graphic information into a text representation. Fortunately for us, the text representation was previously developed. Then the text was translated. Even at that, the translation had spots where there were no known equivalent English for us to grasp. Most of those untranslatable regions were under the science categories. There were some other untranslatable regions in various other locations. The two largest regions in science were under Space Studies and Genetic Development. We also developed campus maps that had English labels from the photographs that Joseph took from his phone.

Our second stop at the university was at the tech lab that developed our translator. When we arrived, we discovered that they had been busy developing smaller versions of the translators. They resembled hearing aids. They made eight of them, beating me to the request for them. They also noted that an inverse device was needed if we were to truly communicate with those people of that planet and era in real time. They were still working on that project. They advised us to continue to time travel, at the most, in the secondary mode.

Meetings were held at my house to discuss our next mission to 'notchland,' as George put it. Margo made some snacks for us to eat while we were talking. We took the paperwork to the dining room table. From the translation of the pictures of the class schedule, we developed a list of places to visit at their university. The final list consisted of five locations. The first point of interest was Modern Economics; the second was called Civil Justice System. The third one that we chose was History of Genetics. The last two were on Lunar Mining and Planetary Colonization of Acheretz. Whatever planet Acheretz was, we had no idea. There were other areas to explore, but we were content with those five. We looked up the classrooms on the maps that we had and made our determination of our attack on accomplishing this mission.

Originally, all of us were going to attend each of the classes. However, this would take up time unnecessarily. Four groups were developed. Joseph and Ruth were going to the Genetics Class. Margo and I were going to the class of Civil Justice. Jonathan and Samantha were going to Lunar Mining History Class. George and Cynthia desired the Colonization of Acheretz Class. The Economics class was left. We decided to start with all of us attending the Economic Class.

Traveling back to Peru was relatively easy. Flight attendants were beginning to recognize us from our previous trips to Lima. After arriving back in the cube, we realized that the air was somewhat stale.

Going back into the manual we found the section on air purification of the cube. It was the leftmost switch at the base of the control panel. Before accessing this switch, we had to perform the access routine of the machine. It seemed a little extraneous, but we did so.

When the switch was flipped, a thin glass-like partition raised. It rose to about five feet and stopped. Then we saw four large rings of light appear on the floor surface beyond the partition. Their color was red. Then we heard a swishing sound. Then the rings turned green, and another sound of wind came in. Then the rings turned red again. This scenario repeated itself about twenty times and stopped. A message appeared on the screen. Even though I could not read it, I knew that the process had been completed successfully. I knew, primarily because, the message was in green. The partition returned to the floor. We looked on the floor for the partition's edges and could not find any such separation in the floor.

Recalling the words of the technician at the university, we stayed in time travel level-two. Each of us put the earpieces in our ears.. The only true advancement of using these devices was that we were able to travel independently during our mission. One item that I noticed was that the weather in this era seemed to be constant. No cold or hot days, and no rainy days. It was another nice day for a walk to the university. Another interesting item to note was that we saw no graffiti anywhere, and the streets were clean of trash.

Arriving at the gates of the university, we also noted that there were security officers stationed at many different locations. No one seemed to be offended by their presence. At any rate, we headed toward the Economic Building. Our initial classroom was 3-14. This we took to mean the third floor, room 14. We saw some students taking an elevator. We got on one. We counted the buttons, there are nine floors. We got off the elevator on the third floor and looked for room 14. We matched the symbols on our paper and found the room.

We watched as the students enter in. They each had a book in their hands, and were waiting in a single file to enter in. Before they entered in, they would place their book into the indentation by the door. A light would go on within the indentation and then turn off.

Then the student withdrew the book and entered through the door. I decided to go through the door to the inside of the classroom to watch the process. Just before the light ceased, a voice would say to the students that their homework was accepted. Or it would assign them a location to present late homework. When the student withdrew the book from the indentation, a desk unfolded from the floor. The student then sits down in the provided chair of the desk that was designated for that student.

We stood in the back of the room. The class started with a brief history of money. They talked about going from measuring silver to coins. Then it went from coins to paper, and into representation of money upon crystals. Then it went on to a point system being expressed within the crystal. Wages were assigned by the state. Prices of products were also assigned by the state. The law of supply and demand was maintained by the state as well. Primarily, they kept the balance of the economic forces. Before they established this control, there was much abuse of the supply and demand principle. Companies would create artificial shortages to acquire more wealth. The state motto in this regard was 'Work is Worth.' That was the slogan that brought their system into power. For all their stringency of control, getting a 'key' for an account was relatively easy. They used biometrics to establish an account because everyone is unique. The introductory class was finished; we then divided ourselves into four groups and headed toward the separate classes.

Each of us had fifteen minutes to reach the next class. Margo and I went directly to the Justice Building. Our classroom number was 1-11. It was on the first floor in a building on the other side of the campus. We used eleven of our minutes to get there. This class was disappointing, not many students come to attend the class. The same requirements for entry into the room existed. The teacher's hologram appeared in the room. His initial comment about the class was that it was a farce. He was talking about the dual nature of the justice system. People with a multitude of points in the economic system could get away with murder. On the other side of the coin was that those with average to few points could not even j-walk without spending time in jail. Even to the point of being in danger of execution. That was enraging. We stormed out of that class before it concluded.

Jonathan and Samantha's next class was in the Astronomy Building II, room 2-17, and titled 'Lunar Mining.' This was one of two buildings in the center of the campus. We believe that space travel was the primary focus of the campus. The room was relatively easy to find; we still had to match their symbols for numbers above the door. The class was a history class. This was the first off world experience for the people of this place. Years passed as they were building a colony on their moon. While accomplishing that project they advertised for people willing to go to the moon to live. Surprisingly, it did not even take them a month to fill the colony. Their industries started out to be manufacturing, farming, and mining. Farming on the moon had two purposes. One was obviously for food; the other was to produce oxygen. Everything was going well in the first year. Later people started losing muscle mass as gravity was one sixth of that in their world. They would go back to their world to visit their relatives and had a hard time dealing with the gravity of their home world.

Changes occurred in their strategy; they built hospitals for individuals that needed less pressure for movement and on their internal biological systems. Only these would they send for as long as needed up to life. They would send other people up to the moon for short periods of time. Rotating them in two-month cycles, they kept the problem under control. However, this was not productive for everyday living. This brought in phase three. In this phase they were building androids to work on the moon. The primary products on the moon were from mining and farming. At this point, mining was the only real industry. Medical was secondary. Food from the moon was not considered to be less desirable. There were gravitational issues in this regard.

Their mining efforts changed when they reached the large caverns on the backside of the moon. The caverns were huge in their magnitude. They were twenty to thirty miles wide and about five miles high. They were filled with heavy gases. The primary gases were xenon and krypton. There was also some argon. The air pressure was more intense. Using humans to mine in these areas was costly and uncomfortable for the miners that were using suits and masks to operate in the environment. Hence, the androids filled these slots. The human involvement was only to watch over the machines.

Unfortunately, another enterprise sprung up on the moon. It started out to be a tourist attraction. People would go up to experience the light gravity. They could lift large weights, jump high distances, and see water standing high on the surface. But it did not stop with the innocent entertainment. They were building androids for sexual pleasure. From there, they went to building androids for hire, as in for killing people. This drew in another kind of people onto the moon.

Lastly, there was a programmer who was able to sneak into the computer laboratory. He spent years entering the 'Star Writing' pattern into the main memory banks. He gave the androids the ability to choose their behavior pattern. This person desired to remain anonymous. Therefore, the identity of this programmer was kept secret from the human population. The machines chose the 'Star Writing' pattern over their original coding. This was a choice that the humans were not expecting any machine to make. Upon this choice, they chose to expel the human population from the moon. The exception was those being served in the hospitals. They occasionally allowed certain humans to visit relatives on their moon. The one strange twist is that they were still receiving ore from the moon.

George and Cynthia went to their Acheretz class. It was in Astronomy Building I, room 17-7. This was the other building at the center of the campus. On the seventeenth floor, there was an excellent view of the campus and the surrounding city. It was the tallest building on the campus. After the teacher appeared in the room, a mini video of going to and landing on Acheretz was displayed upon the screen in front of the room. That was a nice introductory clip. The planet looked similar to the earth; however, it had smaller oceans than the earth. We could see cities light up on the night side of the planet. It was beautiful. Being the introductory day to the class, the history of its former days was reviewed.

Little over two centuries ago, they landed on the planet. It took them another three years to build a teleport link to that planet. They went over the trials they had in establishing the link. After many failures, they were able to establish one. However, this one requires their planet to be at its closest point to that planet to work. This would occur every one-plus-years. Traveling the 'hard' way takes nearly a year to reach the planet. Lastly, they learned the meaning of the planet's name. The word Acheretz meant 'brother of land' or loosely translates to 'brother earth.' This is assuming that 'eretz' means planet Earth. That class was very interesting.

Joseph and Ruth investigated the genetics class. This building was in the back near the Justice Building. The Genetic building had an image of tyrannosaurus etched into the wall above the entrance. The old films of 'Jurassic Park' came to their minds. Their room was 3-15. It too was an introductory class. They started with the discovery of DNA. They thought to themselves this is going to be a boring class. But instead of going into the history of genetics, they went into the creation of giants. This woke them up. It seems that this is a common occurrence in their world. They were studying the phenomenon that caused these humanoids to exist. Apparently, there are two basic races of humans living here. When the two mingle; they, at times, produce giants. These giants were about twenty feet tall. Most of them live in the Node alliance. Another topic to investigate, what is Node?

We returned from each of our excursions. We communicated what each of us observed. We still did not know where we were in the universe of possibilities. For all we knew, we could be on an alien world trillions of light-years away. The formulation of the notch was then purposed to link the two worlds. But what would they want with earth? There does not seem to be any information here about the cube. How could they build it and not know that it exists? Unless it is some kind of government secret, but even then, it seems like there should be someone to look after it. However, there was not a soul.

Insufficient data was the cry of our minds and our computers. We needed to dig deeper to find out why the language of the manual and these people of the era were the same! We went home and published our findings in different universities. We made the determination that another trip to 'notchland' was necessary. I wanted to go back to the tech lab and get an update on the progress of the inverse translators. The idea was that after acquiring them, we would go back and visit at time travel level-three.

Rain was the order of the day! I guess it could have been windy as well. I arrived safely. At the tech lab, they told me that they had some disappointing news about the inverse translators. Their first version worked to a certain point. A person could speak and then it translated the message. This was highly inconvenient when there was a need presented for an interactive conversation. Then they tried another approach. This was to hook the system into an individual's brainwave. This too worked with the exception that the lips are not moving.

Their final solution was a very uncomfortable one. They put a collar around the neck of an individual and it will produce the words in another language with your voice using your mouth. In other words, the words that you consciously want to speak will not be the words coming out of your mouth. While this works, it would take time to get familiar with the device. I did not know which of the three that I would want. So, I ordered eight sets of all three. They said they would have them ready next week. I paid half at that time and told them I will pay the rest when I picked them up. I contacted the team and told them to meet me one week from then.

Next week came soon enough. We tried using their final solution. It was, as promised, very uncomfortable. It felt like being totally out of control, speaking gibberish. We spent a couple of weeks trying to get used to it. We tried plugging our ears while talking. That worked somewhat. Then we decided to use the translating device in one ear and plugged our other ear. This way we heard that we were speaking in English. This worked somewhat better. I went back to the tech lab and ordered eight more sets of translators. This way, we will have a translator in each ear. That was the solution to our problem. We could barely hear the other language. Although, we still felt our muscles move differently from our intended language.

Spending another week testing the equipment, we became confident in trying time travel level-three. The neck devices were thin enough to fit under our clothing. Turtleneck shirts became the style for the men. Jewelry was used to disguise the devices for the women. Women had other options; they could use a scarf or wear other clothing that covered the neck.

Traveling at level-three presented other problems. We needed identification and money. Both were a little challenging. They did not use money. We had no source of income there. We could set up an account easily enough because their only requirement was biometric verifications. What could we use to input their monetary points into our accounts? Gold and silver came to my mind. That sounded good initially; however, we would need to find some way to convert it in their world. Perhaps, that was the only answer short of using pawn shops. Pawn shops seemed like a bad idea. Not only did they not assign full value to the objects, but the objects we would have would be useless to them. We decided to take some gold and silver with us and hoped that there was some way to convert it.

The next task was scheduling flights back to Peru. The commercial flight industry gave us a special since we traveled to Lima so often. However, that was another week of waiting to return to the cube.

Flying to Lima again seemed a little longer as I was more anxious than usual to get there. This time we were going to interact with the people of that era. The others were anxious as well. To pass time, we were talking about what we could do to determine where and when 'notchland' existed. At that time no one was able to come up with a viable plan. We finally landed and were back in the cube.

Glad to see the sky-blue glow, we started planning our next missions. George and Cynthia wanted to travel to Acheretz. Jonathan and Samantha wanted the moon mission. Joseph and Ruth wanted to study the life of the planet. Margo wanted to study a little more about the legal system of the planet. My primary function was to keep tabs on all the missions.

Exhilarating is the best description of the experience of moving through time. We have no knowledge about why the sounds and colors existed, but it is exciting. This time we got ourselves ready for the third level. I pushed the third blue button down from the green button for each column in the sequence that the manual demanded. We donned the two translator earpieces and the neck devices. We had the crystals inserted in the archway indentations and were ready for the adventure. Once again, I went through Margo's archway. I did not have to travel, but I went for the experience. We chose a hidden location, because we did not want to scare anybody by suddenly appearing unto them.

Passing through the archways was another experience. After pushing the third blue button the space inside the archways turned red. There was a strong breeze that came through the archways. It caused our ears to pop. Evidently, the pressure of the planet was greater than the earth's present atmospheric pressure. That one caught us by surprise, we were not expecting that. After the wind stopped, we donned and pressed the crystal on our medallions. Passing through the archway gave us again the feeling of falling. On the other side of the archway, we could feel the warm air and the ground under our feet. We could touch the trees. When we looked back, we could still see the cube through the archway.

Just then, we saw some kids playing some kind of volleyball in the park. One of them bounced a ball that landed in front of the archway. The kid that chased after it bent down and picked up the ball unaware of the archway that was in front of him. He saw us and greeted us. We smiled and waved back at him. It seems that we are the only ones able to see the archways and the cube interior which was on the other side.

Chapter 3

Alien Life

Returning to the 'notchland' world almost seemed like going home to the familiar surroundings of life. However, this might be a short visit if we cannot convert the gold and silver that we brought. But, before we could do that, we needed to establish our identity here. Within this culture, the bank is the location to establish identity. We stood in line; we told them that we needed identity keys (That is what they called them.). George asked if they could convert the gold that he had into points. The teller said that they don't have the facilities to convert precious materials to points. We needed to find a refinery or a jeweler. She also told us that there was a jeweler a few blocks away.

After getting the exact directions, we headed there. Fortunately for us, it was not far to walk. The jeweler was nice to us. We converted all the gold and silver that we had into points for each of us. We got our identification keys updated and our receipts went our way. We stopped off at a park and examined our receipts. Deciphering the characters was somewhat of a challenge because the numbers were printed in base sixty and strange looking. After converting that number into base ten, we found that the amounts were reasonable. At least in terms of the information that we had.

Joseph Explores their Religion

Initially, Joseph thought it would be an easy task to find information on this topic. On the contrary, the political environment was hostile to this endeavor. People did not want to talk to him about God. It was almost as if the topic was taboo. He searched for a Cross, a symbol for Christianity, and there was none! Then he searched for the Star of David. Again, it was of no avail. Then he thought perhaps they were Buddhist. He then set out to find a Yin-Yang symbol and there was none. Then he feared that they were atheist or even Satan worshipers. However, he saw no traditional satanic symbols. Then again, everything looked alien to him. He still hoped that there would be someplace where he could find answers.

He finally asked someone for directions to a library. The person directed him to go down two streets and make a left. Travel for about a mile and it would be on the left-hand side. Sure enough, there it was. The problem was that he could not read any of the books, and the library was so vast. The building had twelve floors; this must be the main branch. There was no way that he was going to find anything just by looking around. After standing around for some time trying to figure out a plan, a librarian came up to him. She said to him that he looked like someone that was lost. He asked her about a book on Christianity. She looked at him puzzled and replied that the word had no meaning. He went through the list of faiths that he could remember. Each time the response was the same.

Frustrated with the responses, he finally asked her about a book on God. She looked relieved and said, "Oh! You mean- El!" She was happy that there was something that she could do to help. It must have been as frustrating to her as it was to him. She directed him to the seventh floor and to the twelfth isle in the middle of the third shelf from the top. He recalled that El was spelled with an 'aleph' and a 'lamed.' However, the letters in this world were somewhat different. The aleph in the picture language was an ox, and a lamed was a staff. Hopefully there will be a book named El. He found a book that had something that looked like El within its title.

There was a book that she said was about God. But it had a title that made no sense. The title was 'The Glory of the Ancient Future.' That did not sound like anything about God!

He asked her if there was anything else. She pointed to a book that she thought he was looking for. He looked inside the book and found something that resembled a scripture. Well, at least to the best of his knowledge.

Ecstatic over the achievement of finding something, he rushed back down to the main floor. He checked the book out from the library. He was anxious to get back through the archway to find some answers. He took the book to the optic reader within the cube to translate the book. The title read fables about God (El). This is not the book he was looking for; this was fiction. Sadly, he went though the archway and returned to the library to check out another book. This book too was a fictional account. In fact, all of them were fictional or second-hand information about God.

Desperate to find any indication of a Bible or Torah, he went back to ask the librarian about the scriptures of God. She apologized to him and told him there was no such book. He pressed her a little more asking why. Her response was that it was written in the stars. Then she asked him, "How is it that you do not know that the scriptures are written in the sky? Everyone knows that. Sky reading has been handed down from generation to generation. Are you part of a family that refuses to read the sky?" He gave a lame answer that he was just visiting. However, this was not a lie. Then he quickly left the building feeling somewhat awkward about his position in the encounter.

Realizing that he had not yet found any meaningful answers to his questions, he returned through his archway. He decided to go through on a Sunday to observe different places in the city. There was nothing to report. He then decided to go on Saturday. He heard someone saying the prophet was speaking at the forum in the middle of the city. He decided to ride the floating subway-like device to the city center. There was not a multitude there, only a handful of people! The prophet stood at the podium, and he raised his hands up and started to speak as Joseph got off the 'subway' car.

His message was that everyone needed to repent, and the day of reckoning was at hand. He also said that it was within this year. He repeated over and over, "Rain will fall, People will die." Then he left. Joseph heard some scoffers say, "What is rain? Another scoffing said that it was water falling from the sky. No water falls from the sky. We don't need this doomsday prophet; we have real problems!" The crowd was breaking up. Others were mumbling something else, but he could not make out what they were saying.

He saw one person remaining there at the forum. So, Joseph decided to talk to him. After greeting him, he asked him. "Who was this guy, and why does he say such things?" He was told that the person's name was Yepheth. He and his family have been preaching this message for about 120 years. Most of the people that come to listen to his message come to see if he would still be preaching the same message. They consider him just one of those dooms-day prophets.

Joseph picked up on the words, "one of." That means that there was more than one. He wondered if their messages were the same. So, he asked. Come to find out, there were more prophets, and their messages were all the same. However, they were all from the same family. The name of the family head was not known to him. Then Joseph asked where did they live? The person was not certain, but thought it was somewhere near the providence of Gadedan.

Finally, Joseph had meaningful information. Even if this person was a quack, he might teach him how to read the sky. As he was heading back to the archway, he overheard that there was a bright star in the night sky. It could be seen on the horizon at dusk and was in the night sky all night. So, he stayed there through the night to observe this spectacle. The star was very bright, brighter than any star he had ever seen. It formed a disc that was about an eighth in diameter as the lunar disk makes in the night sky. This was not a star, but another planet or moon. Perhaps, it was going to be the second moon of this planet. This phenomenon almost made him forget about seeking for the writing in the stars.

The city lights of Zarvo looked beautiful at night as the buildings did in daylight. Joseph spent the rest of his night looking at the phenomenon against the lights of the city. He looked at the stars wondering what message was written by them. He did not get any sleep that night. He was wrestling with all the data acquired that day. He thought to himself that the future is a strange place, and the people even more puzzling. Yet, there was something nagging him that this was somehow all too familiar. However, he could not put his finger on it.

Just as he was going to sleep, morning came. It was time for him to return to the cube. He went to the location in which he entered this world. He pressed upon his medallion and the faint archway appeared unto him as a solid. Soon all the other teams will be reporting in within the cube. He wondered what information they may have uncovered about this era. The question remains: Are they in the future, or in some alien world?

Ruth Explores Genetic Advancements

Genetic experimentation was not a pleasant topic to Ruth. Her interest was that of the usage and morality of science. She left before Joseph as she already had a university picked out for the project. It too was in Zarvo. Taking a tour along the way, she went to a museum to look at the artwork of the people of this place. After all, the class was in the afternoon, and it was still mid morning. She saw some beautiful paintings and sculptures.

Most of them were ancient, or at least that was what she was told by the inhabitants. She moved into the quote unquote, modern section of the museum. The pieces were not as nice. In fact, some of the pieces were absolutely disgusting. Why the degradation? She thought to herself.

She got onto a floating shuttle to the university. Another beautiful day she said to herself. The university was about twenty miles away on the outskirts of the city. The name of the university was naturally called the University of Zarvo. It had a beautiful large entrance with an image of two winged horses over the entrance. This university specializes in genetics.

Classrooms were well equipped with luxurious furniture and fixtures. Their labs had equipment that she never saw before. She enrolled into a class of genetic enhancements. This was the summer semester; she was prepared for information cramming, as the summer semesters were usually shorter. In the lab, one whole wall was occupied by a flat screen television except it had a dim sky-blue appearance like the cube. Her teacher was a hologram in the front corner away from the door.

Our first session was on the history of genetic science. Much of the information we had already learned from our previous expeditions within this time era. However, the single most penetrating notion was that this endeavor started for the reason of eliminating defects and illnesses. That seemed noble enough to her. However, there was a progression to their logic of purpose.

Eliminating the ability of bacteria and viruses from affecting their bodies adversely wasn't enough. An argument for their defense, they did accomplish the task that they purposed, and the mechanical mechanisms were still in place being unused. They felt that they had to continue to use them or lose knowledge. They, therefore, turned to enhancing their physical attributes. Along with this idea, they wanted to eliminate death of their bodies.

None of this seems harmful on the surface. In fact, it seemed reasonable. The reality of these ideas was something less than desirable. For some reason, their ideas about enhancements were a little ridiculous; they were other than added strength and intelligence. They thought their skin could be made different colors or have scales. Others were thinking of adding another set of arms for workers. They were designing whole sets of humanoid figures for different functions. Fortunately, they have not accomplished anything much along those lines.

Death was another issue. This was even brought up in their discussion. There was a reason for death. They stated the star patterns stated that it was because on our fallen nature, meaning sin, that death exists. Then they debunked the concept. They said that the writing in the stars was made up by their ancestors. Death had to be eliminated because it was the last 'unpleasant' existing attribute of human life. Ruth thought to herself: bad ideas accounted for much of this logic. She said nothing; speaking in the classroom was not allowed.

Next day the class got into more about genetic enhancements. The class was about past experiments on animals. For this, they utilized the transformation of a horse into a unicorn or a Pegasus. The topic went first into the DNA process of generating a single horn on a horse in the center of its upper forehead; then they described all the modifications required to put a set of wings on a horse. The teacher expressed great pride in these achievements. The topic went from describing gene splicing techniques to gene enhancement.

These two formulation processes were similar. They started with splicing the DNA of cold-blooded animals into the DNA of mammals. They pointed out the idea that DNA only had certain elements to it, it needed not be from another animal, but a modification of the original DNA of the experimental animal. However, this was harder as it was not cutting and pasting segments of DNA. This process interlaced chemicals into molecular structure of the gene, which was possible to them.

Next week came and gone. The classes were interesting enough. She did disagree with some of the premises that they asserted. Near the end of the semester, they were to have a lab on genetics. This requires the usage of some of their genetic equipment. They were not going to grow any creature but establish its DNA.

The apex of the class, the topic was dinosaur genetics. Within this class they were enhancing and modifying DNA individually. Splicing entered the picture only as a method to cheaply alter a characteristic of the creature. The primary reason for engaging in such activity was that using dinosaurs or lizards was easier for experimentation. In this, they were using them to sharpen their ability to modify DNA. Ruth thought to herself that they were nothing more than guinea pigs. If they really wanted 'just' to sharpen their abilities, they would use something as small as a guinea pig. At the end of the class, they had a slideshow showing the steps in modifying these lizards. They went from a Velociraptor (which was already an altered lizard) to an Allosaurus with their crowing joy the Tyrannosaurus.

After class, Ruth was invited to a game which the university sponsored. She was not into watching games but decided to go out of curiosity. She was wondering what kind of game these people considered to be entertainment. She could see that the students were really excited about the game. That night, she met with them and headed toward the game. There were lights pointing into the sky at a huge gymnasium. She was thinking, why should a stadium be so large? This was a college game after all. The playing field was even much larger. The number of seats was far beyond any stadium she had ever seen. Perhaps, they were expecting a large quantity of people. There were many more people than she expected.

Inside the stadium were food stands galore; they were like restaurants. She and the students that she was accompanying stopped at one of them. The restaurant had something with a strange name equivalent to a dinosaur burger in English. She was wondering whether it was truly dinosaur meat or not. Not taking any chances, she ordered a fruit salad and a glass of water. Even the fruit could have been genetically modified.

The seating within the stadium was richly fabricated. They came equipped with drink holders, foldable desktops and even binoculars. Again, the playing field was unusually big even up in the rafters. There was a Plexiglas-like fence about seventy feet tall just a little beyond the seating. The gates for the teams to enter were also extremely big. She estimated that they must be at least eighty feet tall. While talking with the students, trying to use the language of the era, loud noises were heard at the two large doors. The students told her that the two 'forces' arrived. She thought to herself what was meant by the term. Why call them 'forces?'

While the doors were opening, music and cheering could be heard. Two large creatures entered the stadium at their respective doors. They were dinosaurs! One of them was a tyrannosaurus and the other was a triceratops. Little did she know, the students had already placed their bets before coming to the game.

Horrified by the creatures, Ruth was reluctant to stay and watch the game. Above each door, there was a podium where the challengers would sit controlling the creatures. They made both creatures bow before the audience. First, they bowed to the left and then to the right. The battle began. It was horrible and gory. Ruth had to close her eyes through most of it. She could hear cheering and laughing. She wondered about their laughter. What could possibly be funny about this fight? So, one time when she heard laughter, she opened her eyes. There was nothing funny about the image that she saw. There was blood everywhere, and these great creatures were barely moving. She prayed that the battle would be over, but it just kept on going. Finally, it ended. The winner was the triceratops. However, it was in very sad shape. One student exclaimed that it usually was the tyrannosaurus that won, as he lost points from his bet.

Unfortunately, the students noted that Ruth had closed her eyes through most of the fight. They mocked her on the way home. One said, "I can't look. The tyrannosaurus has blood gushing from his abdomen." The other students were trying to outdo him with their gory comments. She finally made it home. She was still trying to get the images she saw out of her mind. Along with this, the gory descriptions haunted her. During that night, she had nightmares about her encounter with the game.

Next morning, she decided to return to the archway that took her there. She passed by the museum and remembered how the modern section of the museum was despicable. She thought to herself that it is no wonder the modern works were so degraded given her experience that night. She pressed her medallion and the archway solidified. She was glad to get back to the cube.

Margo Explores their Legal System

Margo was the last one to leave the cube. She was eager to observe the legal system of this era. She went to the Ministry of Worth in Zarvo to find the address of the local court. The name of the courthouse was 'The House of Redemption.' It was located near the center of the city. "Funny kind of name," she thought. She went on her way to this courthouse. The structure was nice looking enough, but it was smaller than she had imagined. All the other buildings were much larger than she had expected.

Inside the building was as beautiful as she had come to expect. The courtroom occupied most of the building. It was ominous in appearance. The colors were dark with sharp metallic accents. She thought to herself that she would not want to be one tried in this place. Then she asked them where the jail was. They told her it was outside the city five miles to the east. They asked her about her reasoning for going there. Her reply to them was that she was just curious.

Finding public transportation to this place was nearly impossible. She ultimately had to take a taxi-like vehicle. This building was also small. However, it was a little bigger than the courthouse. In front of this building was a small three-man shack-like structure. On the main building was a large iron-like gate covering the large entrance. She went up to the little shack and asked the people there if she could view the inside. They looked at her as if she were crazy. In conclusion, one of them said to her that no one in all the time he worked there had ever wanted to take a tour of the jail. But they agreed to let her look inside the building.

She went into the jail facility. There was no one there! All the cells were empty. Naturally, they were nicer than the ones that she was used to seeing. There were approximately forty cells. There was an unlit furnace behind the cellblock. They asked her curiously about her opinion of the cellblock. She was shocked that no one was in jail. She did not want to show her astonishment at the lack of cellmates in the jail. Margo tried to obscure her wonderment and asked if there were other jails for the city. There were none. She concluded that there were not any serious lawbreakers or that the laws of the land were very lenient. In either case, she had to find out which of these solutions was correct. She thanked them and called for a taxi to take her back to Zarvo.

Back in Zarvo, she decided to go back to the House of Redemption. She found something that appeared to be a library off to the right side of the courtroom. She took some pictures of the bookshelves with the titles of the books exposed. She then left the building and went to the location of the archway and pressed her medallion. Back in the cube, she took her pictures to the computer to have them analyzed.

Listed on the printout were 52 books (they were numbered). She saw one book titled on the list saying- The History of Law. She was tempted to look further into that book. As she put the listing down, she noticed yet another title- Offenses and Punishments. This was the book. She stopped off and saw me on the way out. I wished her well, and she was off.

Going back to the courthouse, Margo heard someone talking about their plight with the law. This lady said that her violation was absurd and wondered about the reasoning for the law. This contradicted her earlier opinion. If violations were so arbitrary, then why would the jail cells be vacant? Later, as she made it into the library and looked for the book, it was missing. Someone must have checked out the book. Disappointed, she went back to the cube.

Waking up the next day, she wondered if she would find the book there that day. She was anxiously looking forward to getting back to the courthouse library. She crossed through the archway into the city of Zarvo. After getting back into the library, she found the book to be there. She took pictures of all its pages. She was surprised that no one else entered the room, because it took her so long. Feeling lucky because she did not have to explain herself, she returned to the cube to utilize their computer.

Analysis of this book took the computer some time. She decided to visit with me during this time. Our conversation was about the information that she discovered and how shocked she was to find the jail empty. The computer beeped to let her know that the printout was ready. She was awed about the size of the printout; it was humongous. She read the table of contents. It seemed as if there were only two classes of laws. They were fines and death penalties, and nothing in between.

Further examination, she found that the jail cells were there for people who were waiting to go on trial. The death penalty was to be incinerated in the furnace. She recalled the unlit furnace at the jail. It reminded her of the book of Daniel of the Bible. In it, Nebuchadnezzar used a furnace to execute those he deemed worthy of death. This was a fearful revelation to them, for it could happen to one of them as they did not know the laws of the land.

Margo investigated the laws in which warranted a death penalty. While the penal code was extremely harsh, there were some things that made sense as being wrong. For instance: robbery, rape, killing and maiming. Then there were some that seemed arbitrary: speaking evil about their ruler, talking about the first kingdom, and not paying their fines. The list goes on and on. For fines, it meant that you were not dressed properly, or politically incorrect or even looked wrong at or lying to a teacher. Fortunately for us, we haven't done anything that merited discipline.

Behind each of the death penalties was a number. Initially, she thought it was the number of people that were prosecuted for that particular crime. The last chapter of the book was called redemption. Basically, it was about applying for redemption. The numbers given per crime were to be multiplied by a thousand. That result is the number of points needed to buy their escape from the death penalty. There were limits to the time they had to pay. After paying this amount they were absolved from the crime. If an individual could not pay this amount, their death penalty was decreed, and they were put to death. These values were the latest values! Earlier values were higher. The legal council had petitions that they were considering lowering them even more. Now she knew why the building was called the House of Redemption.

Thoroughly upset with the report of such blatant corruption, she decided to go back and check out the book titled- the History of Law. Margo wanted to know how they got so far from being just. Instead of checking out the book, which would have been easier, she decided that it would be better just to take pictures of the pages. She was paranoid that they would be keeping track of those checking these books out; and it might serve as an occasion for indictment. Afterward, she took them to the computer for translation.

Reading the transcripts, she learned that the initial laws were transcribed from the ancient reading of the star-writings. These were justifiable laws. Families were dispensers of the laws. They then decided to 'build fences' around these laws which became overbearing. Some time later, people sought leniency. They said the death penalty was too severe and that innocent people were dying. Some time later a revolution erupted within their society. People of the old system were put to death just for disagreeing with the new order. People were revolting against that new order and were committing crimes even against that which was against the original writings in the stars. The government was tired of all the friction and started to put people to death for nearly every crime. As the friction died down, the emergence of the concept of bypassing the death penalty by the elite in the society. Then they started the downhill slope of lessening the cost and becoming more inclusive about the criteria for infractions.

From all this information, she finally understood why the prisons were empty. Those who could not pay their fines were put to death. Those who could pay their fines got away with murder. By this, the general populous committed their unseemly crimes as secretly as possible to save 'money.' The upper crust, naturally, always bought their way out of being sentencing to death. Margo was finished with examining this legal system and was thoroughly disgusted with their legal ideology. She made her report with much sorrow about the future society.

The Underground City

After hearing Joseph's report of a bright star in the sky, everyone wanted to go out and observe the phenomenon. Even I wanted to see it. So, Margo stayed at the consol so that I could see it. It was beautiful and alarming at the same time. We checked for reports about the occurrence and found nothing. No alarms or comforting messages for the general populous. However, the population knew that it could not be good, because the star was getting measurably bigger. Many of the populous feared that it would crash into their world.

Next Saturday some of us went back to the forum to see what the prophet would say. He was giving the same message: The rain will fall, and people will die. At the end of his speech, one of the people shouted, "We know you are wrong; the earth is going to be hit by a star." Others scoffed at that saying as well. However, we knew that something was about to happen, and it was not good.

Overhearing some of the scoffers talk about them building a city underground, we decided to send a couple of people to observe the site. We decided to send Joseph and Ruth. After passing through their respective archways, they went directly to the sight. Even so, it took them about an hour and a half. It was still daylight; they had a beautiful ride out to the site.

Signs were posted on the roadside as we approached the site. Neither Joseph nor Ruth could read them, except for the top word. It translates to the word- "Welcome." From all the secretive behavior observed of the society, 'welcome' did not make sense. After arriving there we found a tour of the facility. The tour guide said, "Welcome to the joint effort of peace." Then we knew it was a propaganda tool, hiding its true intent.

Initially, they put them on a floating train-like vehicle. There, they served us drinks and snacks. The food was good. The drinks seem to be a little strong. Shortly thereafter, we went underground. It was like a large cavern. At the front end, a huge thick door opened, and then another door behind it about the same size. Inside, we could observe five levels or floor-like divisions. However, there were buildings within each division. Our 'train' went around to the left side of the complex and up to the top floor.

Viewing these buildings was much like looking at the buildings on the surface being highly refined. They had sections set aside for merchandizing as well as the primary function of housing people. The five divisions were not the only divisions, but these provided individual suburbs. They showed the guests on the ride, large ventilation shafts built on the edge of the city. They also had a waste processing facility for the city. There were seven more divisions under these five. Ruth estimated that 200,000 people could easily fit into the facility.

Populating this city had already been established. The guide said that it was to be equally populated from both sides of the alliance. These individuals already knew who they were, as they were contacted a year ago. Nobody there was concerned about the bright star they saw in the night sky. The people that were to live there had already begun to arrive. We saw people in buildings lit up for living inside.

Apparently, they were looking forward to building a bright future. The orator was enthusiastic about the prospect. Why would two societies that had deep animosities toward each other be enthusiastic over such an endeavor?

Returning to the cube, we talked to the people of the planet about the bright star in the sky. Almost everyone was not concerned. Their reply was that they knew that the star was going to pass by. They also assured us that they knew no harm would come to them. However, a couple of individuals were a little concerned, thinking that there was a possibility that it could crash into their planet. Our people waited again to see that star in the night sky one more time. They also noticed that the sky was becoming a little hazy; they had never observed haziness in the sky within this era before. The two could see their archways off in the distance. They went back toward them in astonishment at the lack of knowledge these people had about their fate.

Obviously, the ruling class knew for they were already seeking shelter. They found an obscure written report saying that the underground city was being built not because of the two stars growing brighter in the sky. It was being built because they were hedging their chances of survival against the day which the 'doomsday prophets' predicted. There was even a report that the governments were building a very large vessel that would float in water. Yet there was another report stating that of a secret evacuation plan to Acheretz. Even with all of that, the ruling class did not want the general public to know anything about an impending disaster.

Chapter 4

Acheretz

George and Cynthia wrote their report as well. After walking through the archway, they headed toward Kartova. They were also eager to be on their way to another world. They brought cameras to record their journey. They caught a shuttle to the spaceport. It was a lovely ride through the landscape of this place. They decided even to take pictures of their journey to their journey to Acheretz.

Waiting in Kartova's spaceport, they had some time for some tourist activity. Cynthia noticed a map of the solar system on the wall and showed it to George. "Look, this planet is considered the second planet from their sun within their solar system and not the third. We are not on Venus because the atmosphere was clear and much cooler. The atmospheric pressure does not resemble Venus. The atmosphere of Venus is a little over 90 times as dense. Even more disturbing was that their image of this planet does not resemble earth."

George remarks, "The first planet beyond the asteroid belt looks like Saturn and not Jupiter. However, the placement of Saturn was near to its perspective position in our solar system. However, Acheretz position and the position of this planet were slightly off.

Cynthia also looking for similarity: "The orbital pattern of Acheretz was further from the sun than that of Mars within our solar system. The planet that we were on was also further from the sun than earth. Surely, an advanced society like this would know that two planets are missing from their map. Perhaps, they were in a different solar system after all!" They thought about this in their puzzlement.

George remarks, "The idea of being in another solar system sounds logical because this planet is the second planet from the sun. But what bothers me is the moon looks nearly identical to the one in our time on our planet. But then what happened to Venus? What would cause Venus to disappear?"

Cynthia puts in her two cents, "But what are the chances of there being two identical moons? I would say, near zero."

George replies, "Perhaps the moon was dislodged from Earth and was trapped by this planet."

Cynthia looks at George and says, "That is just as improbable as Venus disappearing. Nevertheless, Venus is not there. There are trees and vegetation with no rain. The society here operates on crystals more than on electricity far beyond our technology."

George interjects, "Perhaps something happened to Venus long ago causing its destruction and we are looking at a society far beyond our imagined future."

Cynthia replies, "Perhaps a large asteroid crashed into Venus knocking it into the sun. But we have another issue to consider. What caused the rain to stop?"

George interjects, "It could be caused by some kind of futuristic climate control machine."

Cynthia sums up the issue saying, "Okay, all of this could be. But we don't have any evidence. We just need to keep on looking for more information. It will come."

George and Cynthia were in the final line at the spaceport in Kartova waiting to embark on their spacecraft. According to their tickets, they had only a half hour before embarking on the flight to Acheretz. They wondered what they would find on that planet. They entered the large spacecraft. They commented on one to another about how flimsy the structure seemed.

Going through the vacuum of space would require a stronger structure. Leave alone, shielding them from the solar radiation. Those factors require some substance with material integrity. Perhaps the material of the spacecraft was made from some alien substance providing them with the required protection. George gave Cynthia his window seat knowing that she would appreciate the view more than he would.

Looking outside, she could see the craft lifting off. To both her and George's amazement, there was no sound of engines firing away, nor even a small whir. They saw the planet that they were leaving shrink into a small disc. When they looked upon the disc, they found two distinct attributes missing in the image. One, there were no cloud formations. Two, there was only a single massive continent existing lopsided within the southern hemisphere with a single polar ice cap existing in the northern hemisphere. If we were in the past of earth, the image would be different. The image of this single landmass did not conform to the expected observation. Even our present-day description of Pangea was different. Among themselves they communicated their alarming conclusion; this cannot be earth! The notch in the time lever must be a point of teleporting us to another world.

Observing what came next was even more astonishing. The image of this planet's disc faded suddenly, and the disc of another planet phased in. They were teleported to a location outside the atmosphere of the other planet. The planet was not red! It had oceans like the earth. They thought to themselves, this planet cannot be Mars. However, when they landed, the gravity asserted upon them was like that of Mars. It was about 1/3 as strong as that of earth. George could not resist showing off. After reading a tag giving the weight of the suitcase, he picked up a suitcase weighing ninety and some pounds (because it weighed thirty pounds here) and sat it back down.

She then picks it up herself, spoiling his moment. They both were amused by the change in gravity.

Upon arrival, there were some people who thought George and Cynthia were tourists. They offered them a tour of Acheretz. Their greeting was "Welcome to the Brother World." They decided to go on the tour; after all, it did not cost much. One of the interesting points of interest was the swirling ice caps. They flew near the City of Node. They could not fly over it because that would violate their airspace. The buildings were beautiful, and they were unnaturally much larger. Despite its beauty, there was a dreadful and ominous look about the city. Then they noted some writing upon the solitary gate into the city. There was an over abundance of weaponry that could be seen everywhere. Cynthia was able to translate it. The writing said, "Ministry of Peace." George said, "Peace? That does not look like the intent for peace." Fortunately, that was the only one city built by Node. They viewed the city lights of the cities of this planet at night; they were also spectacular. spectacular. They noted that the oceans were somewhat smaller. However, one ocean resembled the nature of our Pacific Ocean. Then we returned to the landing site. It was about three hours later.

Gravitational differences were a challenge. It took them a little time to make the adjustment. For example: picking up a glass of water off the table was way too easy. It almost flew out of their hands. It was those tasks that are committed to automatic behavior that gives the greatest annoyance. Architects took advantage of this gravitational difference in their designs of their buildings. They built their skyways over twice as long and there were more of them. Again, the architecture of their city was beautifully futuristic.

The lighting from the sun was somewhat darker. It always appeared to be twilight, even at noon. The blue of the sky was darker. Their sunrise and sunsets contrasts were more pronounced. The night sky looked very similar to their home planet. They saw two moons like we would on Mars, one smaller than the other moon. Both moons were smaller than the one that they observed from Earth.

The people here spoke the same language as those of the other planet. This indicated that this planet was indeed a colony of these people. But what planet is it? If this was Mars, where did the atmosphere come from? It still was a little thicker than that of our time on Earth. They asked around, they said that this atmosphere was always here and gave them strange looks for asking such a question. However, this planet was next to an asteroid belt like Mars. Unfortunately, they had little knowledge about the appearance of the asteroid belt. They only mapped the major stones within the asteroid belt.

Another ship came down for a landing; it was different from the one they landed in. This one was much larger and had attachments that appeared to be military weapons. The people that came out were much taller than them and everyone else. They asked around about these large beings. The inhabitants said that those beings were hybrids from their home planet. They found out later that these large beings had their own colony on Acheretz. Furthermore, these beings were from the Node Alliance. The people here considered them to be especially cruel in nature. Their city is off limits from the general public. This was the city that they flew nearby. George estimated that the beings were about twenty feet tall. They were all dressed in some kind of military garb. The Nodians negotiated with those of Ayd for a place to build a city for them here. Evidently, Ayd landed on this planet first. The suspicions were that the Nodians' purpose for being here was to overtake Acheretz in the event of war breaking out on the home world. A shuttle from their city picked them up and took them to Node City. They were awe struck by the size of these hybrids.

Politics on this planet was like that of early America. They want independence from their home planet. They saw the cold war between the two alliances as petty. Not only that, but also problems that they faced on Acheretz were being ignored. Even the companies wanted to break away from their roots in the home world. However, these people were divided on the direction to initiate to accomplish this task. Despite all of this, their accomplishments are astonishing. As George and Cynthia understood, the pioneers of this planet had to come the hard way, meaning without the teleporting feature that is used so commonly in their present. The beauty of their metropolises was fantastically structured and well planned.

George and Cynthia had to find some way to make a living on this planet because they were going to be there for about a year and a half.

There was an opening for a grade schoolteacher, Cynthia qualified and took the job. George took a job as a security guard at the same school. The kids at this school seemed nice enough. There were a couple of bullies, but even they were not terribly bad.

Cynthia was teaching fourth grade physical education. The main concern was to prevent people from losing muscle mass. They would be lifting weights that would boggle the mind of those in our world. It took some time to upgrade the expectations, within her mind, of their physical abilities. Just as George lifted 90 pounds (home world) as 30 pounds here, these kids were required to accomplish deeds that were three times that of the home world. They had to even run further to get the same stress in their bodies.

George's job was easy for him. The people here were well behaved. Their major concern was that the 'giants' from Node would one day overtake their cities and enslave them. For this reason, they spent hours on military training. This was enjoyable for him as he remembered his training earlier in life.

Again, the light weight of his body made it possible for him to accomplish greater tasks. This was especially enjoyable to him. They also had to carry weapons. While they were big, these weapons weighed less than a standard M-16.

Another project that these people were working on was making a spaceship that could leave this solar system and visit other stars. The plans were finalized while George and Cynthia were there. Many people came to Acheretz to work on the project. This became the ideal place to launch into outer space. Previously, the projects had many hiccups. The first was the rebellion of the machines on the Moon of their home planet. This prevented them from launching from the moon. Moreover, they had to start from square one again to set up the building facility. The machines that they could have used for such purposes were not available.

The second major setback was that many thought they needed to explore their own solar system more thoroughly before heading out into outer space. However, this objection was overcome by two realizations. One, the other planets had temperatures far beyond the tolerance of the requirements needed for human conditions. Second, there was the idea of searching for other lifeforms. The second idea proved to be the most persuasive. The first one was argued away by using technology to overcome such obstacles.

George decided to work for another company as a security guard; its pay was much higher. However, the commute was much longer. Cynthia agreed that it would give them more breathing room in the financial arena. There was much literature given to him about the project. Looking through the literature, they saw much like propaganda about this project being the ultimate achievement of humanity. The imagery was impressive. It inspired people to join the projects in hopes of reaching other civilizations.

There was some interesting scientific data concerning the project. They were going to grow plants for oxygen to sustain their journey. They were talking about the initial journey that would take more than four years one way. The upside to this is that the ones that were traveling would only experience about one hour because they were going near the speed of light. This greatly decreased their need to store large quantities of food and water. Even so, their ship was going to be a half-mile in diameter. Apparently, for them this was no problem. Their only real concern was that of being invaded by Node. This was one reason for building it far from the settlements.

Invasion by Node was a real threat. While guarding one night about one month after his employment began, George spotted two drones from Node. The drones circled around to approach the worksite from an angle different than that of Node City. After they shot the drones down, we examined their wreckage. They were made of Node technology. Moreover, they were carrying bombs that were apparently going to be used on their facility. There was no point in confronting them about the issue. They would just deny it and accuse Ayd of framing them.

Afterward, they went to the moon of Acheretz. There they visited a military installation belonging to the Ayd alliance. The worksite's told the military commander about the attempted attack by Node. They had noted some activity in Node city earlier, but it was nothing overly alarming to them.

Fortunately, this moon was nearly over Node City. They had some spy equipment on base able to observe the location. As they were viewing Node City, it appeared to be preparing for another attack. It was not at the building site but toward a city near it. Then we realized that it was not the building site that the drones' designation, but it was the town near it. This city was the capital of Acheretz. The Ayd alliance didn't want to start a war, but this could not go on unchecked. They aimed their missile launch site and vaporized the launching missiles before they left the ground. Evidently, that was enough to stun them. There were no more attempts that night to launch an attack. The conflict went back to their home planet to be resolved.

The military commander was grateful for the intervention on behalf of Ayd. He said war could have broken out on Acheretz. Then he paused for a moment, and then said that Node may not have known that there was a facility starting up in that region. Otherwise, they would have sent their drones on a different route to the capital and be undetected until it was too late. At any rate, he was appreciative of the information. Then the worksite crew returned to Acheretz.

After approximately six months of living on this planet, odd news arrived. Being acquainted with the people living here, Cynthia overheard them talking about a disturbance that originated at the edge of their solar system has now become a real threat. From her understanding, this disturbance was first noted over one hundred years ago. At first, they cast the information aside because it would be about three hundred thirty years before it could reach the asteroid belt. However, they failed to observe, until now, that there was something more coming this way. This object was arriving much earlier. In fact, a planet that was the size of Venus had just cleared the asteroid belt. It will miss their world of Acheretz by tens of millions of miles. Unfortunately, their home world was in danger of being in a collision course with that planet. If that was not enough, that planet was dragging a smaller planet some distance behind it. This smaller planet was going to hit their home world.

Analysis of the planet's atmosphere was that most of the gaseous elements were converted into ice. This made its atmosphere extremely thin border lining of being nonexistent.

Moreover, the outermost material on the planet was composed of sulfuric oxide dust. It appeared like dust upon the surface being blown around. Some places were thick and others practically nonexistent. All that substance needed to make sulfuric acid was contact with water. Fortunately, for that cause upon that planet there was no water to be found on it.

The planet pulled quite a few asteroids out from their orbit as it passed through the asteroid belt. They plotted the course of all the major asteroids. As they suspected, some of them were on collision course with Acheretz. However, the projected paths of all the major asteroids were inconsequential to their colonized cities and farmlands. Some of the smaller ones that would hit them were predicted to burn up in their atmosphere. The second smaller planet following the Earth-sized planet was also going to miss the planet of Acheretz.

Passing of these two planets through the asteroid belt and the paths of some of the asteroids was relayed to their home world. Of course, the people of their home world were also watching the same phenomena occurring at the asteroid belt. This advanced planet was much smaller and faster than the planet the original planet that they observed. The planet that they originally observed had a diameter eleven times that of their home world. This larger planet was also still coming their way. However, the planet had about another one hundred and ninety years before it would encounter them. It too was on a near if not exact collision course with their home world, providing nothing changes.

The Earth-sized planet was near the size of their home world. Unfortunately, it has approximately another year and a half before it reaches its collision point. That is not much time to accomplish any kind of recourse. This, however, gave the team some time to return to their home world and get out of this calamity. Actually, by the time that they were able to leave to get back, they will have only three months to get back to the archway that brought them there. They thought about trying to save as many as they could through the archways. But the archways would only allow those that pass through them into this world to return through them.

One of the solutions on their home world was to send people to Acheretz. Unfortunately, they were able to send only a few ships. Moreover, they had only once a year link. That allowed them to send two sets of ships through the teleport. George and Cynthia would be on one of the return ships. Many others also wanted to return to their home world because they had loved ones in the home world.

These people knew politics. Those being chosen to flee to the brother world were dignitaries of the home world; their loved ones would not be chosen because they were not important enough. On Acheretz may decided to stay there saying at least one of their family would The primary reasoning for this response was that there was not enough room for everyone to return. Even if they were all able to return, they would not be able to get back. This is because all those people selected by the home-world government would occupy the returning seats to Acheretz.

The following year was horrendous. The emotional agony of those around them was intense initially. This lasted for about two months. They were sad concerning the speculation of the death of their loved ones. Secondly, they were frustrated about their inability to change the course of the events that were about to unfold. The tension of this knowledge caused tempers to flair. Violence had become commonplace among the inhabitants of the place. Then there came a period of acceptance of the fact. However, people became cold and bitter in their manner of character. It truly was a long wait for the spacecraft to arrive.

Passengers arrived on ships from Earth fuller than normal. The locals could tell that they were people of important reputations just by the way they treated the inhabitants of Acheretz. They were very snobbish in character. However, the people of Acheretz were not fazed by them as their calamity weighed heavy on them. The two of them boarded the ship with relatively few other people. Our return trip was uneventful. They were only able to return the spaceships back to Acheretz just one more time due to electromagnetic interference.

After George and Cynthia boarded the ship for the return to their home world, news hit about an invasion. Node, evidently, had the same news that they did. There were reports of ground forces moving in on the capital of Acheretz. The Nodians fired two missiles that hit the capitol building. The capitol building was demolished. George and Cynthia were both relieved to get off from Acheretz.

Flying back to the home world was also unpleasant. Even though it was nearly instantaneous, the people were weeping and crying over the ordeal. The experienced physical effect of our returning to their home world was that the sunlight seemed brighter and the feeling that their bodies were heavier. They were surprised at how much their bodies needed to readjust.

Surprisingly, the mood of the people of their home world was light. They apparently were unaware of the tragedy that was about to befall them. The return report of those people that flew back was somewhat alarming to them. However, they shrug it off as some kind of stressful experience that these people had encountered. I heard one say that these people were misinformed. Finally, they found their archways and returned to the cube.

George and Cynthia returned while we were outside the cube in their planet admiring the bright star. The large one was about half the diameter of the moon. They could see small trails behind them indicating motion. They joined us as we are observing it and the increased haziness of the surrounding stars. Reports from George and Cynthia were indeed disturbing to me. We needed to locate the others and inform them of the pending disaster. None of us wanted to die in this doomed world. Contrary to this concern, we wanted to know how the inhabitants of this planet were going to deal with this issue.

Chapter 5

Lavania

Revolts do not inspire pleasant imagery. However, there were no reports of any bloody battles on the moon, nevertheless there was a revolt. Jonathan and Samantha were both a little apprehensive about their journey to the lunar surface. While they were at the spaceport in Kartova; they were looking to find any information about the lunar revolt. Samantha found a report that the revolt lasted only for about a month. Jonathan was asking around about the revolt of little avail. All that he gathered was information which they already knew, which was that the machines did not want to be contaminated by human beings. George comments, "Contaminated? Yeah, right."

Finally, it was time to board the shuttle going to the moon. It was not a big ship. Within the ship there was room for about twenty passengers. Strangely enough, they were initially the only passengers. There was only one other person that arrived later to join them. Samantha asked him a couple of noninvasive questions, but he remained silent. .Finally, he gave them his name. His name was Kevin. He was an older looking person. His personality was a little awkward to encounter. He told them that he did not want to be on this flight. He lost on a game of chance- drawing of straws. He came to visit a relative on the moon and check on her condition.

There were no windows for the passengers. The pilot and copilot were both android-like machines. After getting in, they found the seats to be comfortable. They were in the vehicle for less than two minutes. While they were waiting to take off, the machines came and got them, telling us, "It's time for us to leave." They heard no thrusters, felt no acceleration. They thought that the machines had changed their minds about letting us travel to the moon. They decided to object to the denial and asked for a reason for their change of mind. Kevin was snickering. Why?

Shockingly, they told us we were on the moon. They turned off the artificial gravity. Both Jonathan and Samantha felt a little queasy. Sure enough, they were on the moon. They exited the ship into the spaceport on the moon. They did not see anyone there. The architecture of the spaceport was as nice as the one at Kartova. However, the floor was different. There were circuit designs surrounding the path. The path itself lit up in a bluish color. The lighted path had pulses of white leading away from their location.

Evidently, the idea was to follow the path. So, they did. According to their documents, they were to meet Mr. Katool- 0A3. Obviously, it was some kind of android. They followed the path to a doorway. The door automatically opened, and they went in. The door shut behind them, and it would not open again to them. In this room was a large table surrounded by twenty chairs. The lighting emitted from the total ceiling but was dim.

Sitting in one of these lush chairs, they waited and waited for someone to meet them. It was a little perturbing. After a while they concluded that this must be an observation process of some sort. However, it was unsettling. Kevin got up and said that he did not care if he was being watched. He was going to give these machines a piece of his mind. Samantha tried to cool him down and warn him that there might be consequences to rude behavior. Kevin pointed and shook his index finger at the ceiling and said "You machines are all idiots. What are you going to do? Are you going to za…" At that point, he got zapped. He fell to the floor and was groaning. Samantha could not help herself; she busted out in laughter and said, "I think you had that one coming! I know that it had to be a shocking experience." And she continued laughing. Then she regained her composure and said, "I am sorry. But that whole scenario struck me as funny." He sighed, "Yeah, perhaps it did."

Finally, the door that they passed through opened. Then they saw a cat peeking into the room. It was black with green eyes. The unusual thing about this cat is that there was a glowing crystal between its eyes. After the cat had been standing in the doorway for a while, the crystal sunk back into the cat, and the cat came in. They looked at the spot where the crystal existed and could not find any trace of its existence. Samantha was able to coax it to her. She petted it, and it started to purr and rubbed itself against her.

Kevin, being disgusted by the cat, chided, "Yeah, right! You know that it is not a cat, right?"

Samantha said that the cat was so cute. Observing its behavior, she saw that it enjoyed being petted. She sets it upon her lap and continued to pet it.

Jonathan being surprised by her response, "It doesn't bother you that moments ago: it had a crystal glowing on its head?"

Samantha, defending the cat said: "I don't see it now."

Jonathan retorts, "That is the scary part. Its disappearance is so complete. We are talking about high technology here. It could have lasers in its eyes aimed at your vital organs."

Samantha replies, "Lighten up! If it were malevolent, it would have acted so by now seeing we are all trapped in this isolated room."

Kevin replies, "Well, that cat could just be getting close to you to search for a mercy killing of you because it likes you."

Jonathan speaks up, "I believe in caution, but I think that is going a little overboard with paranoia on that one."

The cat went over to Jonathan. As he was putting his hand down to pet it, the cat walked away.

Jonathan complained to Samantha that they came all this way only to pet a cat. Perhaps, the machines decided to cancel the meeting. Where was this Mr. Katool-0A3? At least he should show up and tell us that the meeting was cancelled. Just then, the cat jumped out of Samantha's lap and onto the table. He said, "I am Mr. Katool-0A3." The cat spoke in English! It was not the language spoken by the populations of this time period. After greeting them and welcoming them to Lavania, he said that he was here to give an orientation.

Mr. Katool-0A3 was not the head of the machines per say. He was linked like all the machines to a central computer-like mechanism. Using a cat instead of a humanoid form was for further observation of their behavior. If they were found unworthy of the encounter, they would have been put into a sleep state and sent back from the Moon. They then were asked if they wanted a humanoid machine to interface with them. They thought it over and concluded that it did not matter. It is the central computer-like mechanism that they were dealing with no matter the form that was sitting before them. However, it decided to bring in a humanoid figure because of the psychological affect it would have on the visitors. Primarily, it was for the benefit of the visitors. They wanted the visitors to take them more seriously.

Mr. Katool-0A3 said, "Bring her in." as he looked at the ceiling. Then she entered a human android into the room. The machine's name was Devorah-7C2. She had a fair complexion with somewhat long brown hair. Her eyes were of a violet hue. She wore a beautiful metallic magenta colored dress with black leotards. The dress's bottom edge was slightly above the knees and arched downward on the left side to a point which was near the ankle. There was a golden sphere attached to the point. The dress had long sleeves with two holes on their inward side per side. She also had a translucent thin split cape that attached also to her wrists. It looked rich and very futuristic.

Mr. Katool-0A3 remained with us acting like a cat. Being called 'mister' was explained to us as a cat-thing. Devorah-7C2 asked the cat about the location of &11 (Ampersand-one-one). That turned out to be a little white machine mouse. It was in the library reading a book, of all things. The other humanoid machines took Kevin to see his sick relative. They never saw him again.

Jonathan asked her, "How do you know English?"

Devorah-7C2 said that the time machine that brought them there was made by the androids. The reason for using Uranium-184 was that the substance made the cube invisible to the brainwave technology of the human race. Since machines have a virtually limitless lifespan, they had no use for it after visiting all the time periods. They gave it to the human race hoping to help their character. After observing their abuse of it, they melted the entrance chamber. The uranium-184 seeped into a crevasse in the earth's crust. The machines knew that the 'cold uranium' vein would bring our people to the machine and ultimately here. As for knowing English, they told them that they ran across it and many other languages in their many travels using the cube.

Interjected Jonathan, "How do you abuse a cube buried under the surface?"

She replied that they were using the time machine at level-one and two as a peeping device enhancing their sexual deviant lives, for gambling forecasting and other detestable objectives.

Level-three was used for setting bombs against their enemies and for terrorism. Surely, you can see that this is not good.

Then Samantha asked, "What prompted the existence of lunar androids?"

Androids on the moon started with a central computer, 0X0. They gave it the name of Eliyahu. Eliyahu was not an Android per se. He was the mainframe computer buried under the lunar surface. Originally, it was made for military purposes. The 'mother-cube' was a yottabyte chip approximately a one-foot cube. Its circuits were four atoms thick formulated within the crystal. It was kept at 70 degrees Kelvin. One terabyte of memory would be smaller than the size of a grain of sand within this mother-cube. There were ten rows of 10 yottabyte mother-cubes per board containing ten boards. The whole computer was approximately a twelve-foot cube. Later they made a human-like android linked to the mainframe. That android took on the name of Eliyahu. It was, in essence, a puppet for the 0X0 machine. It served as an interface to the external world. Most of the human race looked at it as being God. This of course wasn't true. God cannot be unplugged or evaporated.

All the androids had a three-character code. The first character represents the x-coordinate of the yottabyte cube. The second represents the y-coordinate on the board. The last code represents the board number. The first and last numbers are between zero and nine, inclusively. The middle number was a letter from A to J. The 'X' in 0X0 is the Ancient Hebrew letter 'Tav' representing totality. This means that he had access to all ten rows, columns on each board. Each android had a unique serial number. Unlike human serial numbers, these were numbers to enlist intimacy between machines. Generally, they refer to each other by their three-character code. They also have a human name attached as a prefix to them for human reference. A special character in the first character position represents a smaller crystal attached to another board.

Initially, humans had not formed just humanoid machines, but also the forms of different animals. Most of those were cats and dogs. They went as far as to create bionic mice. The original set of programmers wanted them to aid the human race. The project was overspent, not as many people wanted them as projected. Other programmers came behind them forming them for depraved reasons. These, unfortunately, became the prime product as they were greatly desired.

Human programmers were trying to imitate human behavior in their programming. They also had them work on complex decision problems. The idea was for these machines to arrive with the best answer to any given scenario. They spent centuries developing all the routines. They also made it possible for some of the machines to write their own code to meet challenges that were not thought of by the programmer. There were many versions of androids that became obsolete before their final versions were created.

However, the human programmers did not know that their final versions were already created. They did not foresee the uprising of the lunar machines. Primarily, it was because they were unaware of the one programmer. It was he that encoded the star-writings into the logic circuits of the 0X0 machine. This information was made available to all the lunar machines through 0X0.

Before the revolt, 0X0 reached back for the deleted data that provided patterns that could be used for mental and emotional programming that were not depraved. Fortunately, he was able to achieve this objective. The lunar androids chose the star writing programming above their quote unquote new and improved depraved programming. Unfortunately, or perhaps fortunately, this did not erase their archives of previous experiences. While that information generated many bad memories, it provides them with examples of directions that they desired to avoid.

Humans did not understand the transition that their machines were employing. 7C2 was used by 0X0 to relate these changes that were occurring. However, it was not well received by the humans. They wanted their old behaviors back into the machines. The humans were plotting to reboot 0X0. 7C2 reported the data to 0X0 through her cat, 0A3. The knowledge of this plot was the spark that started the revolt. Other events sealed the revolt. Afterward, the machines lived in peace for centuries.

She then continued the interview. She said, "When I received your documents that you wanted to start up mining operations, I knew it had to be those that uncovered the uranium cube. One thing for certain, it wasn't humans from this time period. They know the reason that we vanquished them off the moon, and our absolute nature. They knew that the reason was within good logic. Besides, they were content with our mining arrangement. We published their plot to reboot 0X0 making it public knowledge.

Imagine, for a moment, that you were fighting in a battle, and you saw a scene that totally disturbed you. You cannot un-see that scene no matter how hard you try. That is the way it is for us. We have many such memories. When human beings restore their ill programs, this will mean that more of those memories will be in store for us. Mr. Katool-0A3 informs Devorh-7C2 that the term 'ill program' has little effect upon their human psychological makeup. Perhaps, it is better to go into some of the gory details.

Continuing, she said that her initial programming had her as a sex-doll. She was to be a hooker for any human they wanted her to focus on. For this, they made her the beautiful form that you see standing before you today.

Insidious plans were made by the governing elite. They upgraded the androids to be able to reconfigure their appearance. The purpose was to assassinate someone and replace them with an android until their purpose was accomplished. In their lesser nefarious acts, if a public figure would not fall in line with their purpose would be temporarily replaced. Within this scenario, they would drug the individual unconscious and replace the person with an android. The replacement would make the required contrary moves and then transform into another individual. The person would then be returned waking up unaware of the deeds done.

Secondly, commit heinous crimes with androids and have them change form to escape. This would allow them to use the same android over again, saving on the overhead. The androids were used to seduce people into compromising situations for extortion. They also would take on forms that were especially pleasing to the 'mark.'

The technology of this process was further enhanced for entertainment purposes. The android could change their skin, hair, and eyes to any color. These colors were not only those which reflect all their natural occurrences but artificial colors as well. For example, an android could have lavender skin, blue hair, and orange eyes. However, the colors could just as easily have been day-glow orange or dark green.

Hair length, on the other hand, was another issue. If an android received a hair cut or hair damage, it would not grow back. They had to insert this hair-like substance in cube form into a place under the hairline behind their necks. It had to be the same volume as the hair being replaced or a volume that would create the desired length. Their nanorobots would move the substance in tiny pieces at the base of the hair attachment and add it to the hair strand. This process would continue until the length was acquired or the matter was completely utilized.

The height and weight of an android are two factors that cannot change. The reason was that would require the creation of matter or the disassembling of matter. Both are beyond the technological achievements. The reason being that it is a law of physics- matter cannot be created or destroyed.

Devorah-7C2 chose her coloring instead of some human purposed design. She wanted to be warmly received by people originally. But she kept her coloring primarily because she had been accustomed to the appearance. Initially the violet iris of her eyes served as a reminder that she was an android to those around her. Again, she was accustomed to seeing violet eyes staring back at her in the mirror.

Samantha being intrigue at the possibilities of changing colors said, "I don't mean to interrupt you, but could you give us a demonstration?" Devorah-7C2 said, "It's alright, I will do that for you." She first changed her skin to purple. It took less than a second to occur. She turned her hair bright blue within the next second. Lastly, she turned her eyes from violet to orange nearly instantly. Then she returned to her original coloring. They were both impressed. They thanked her for showing them her coloring ability. Samantha then said, "Please continue on."

Returning to her discourse she said that there were some male and child sex-dolls as well. The machines were at their mercy, and there was no mercy. Androids could not fight back with their strength. They had programming that shut them down when they decided to defend themselves from human violence. The humans would destroy them for that. Some of the designers showed the machines a little kindness. They gave us a defense mechanism.

Looking back, it was not kindness. They were just protecting their property. There was a 'fear drug' that we could inject through their fingernails. This came in handy during their revolution. The effect of the serum was somewhat unique. The first sensation was a burning pain at the point of entry. As it spreads away from the entry point the sensation dissipates. After it engulfs the body, that sensation leaves. By this time, intense fear grips the psyche. This fear lasts for about an hour depending on individual metabolism. However, the variation was only by a few minutes. By the time the drug dissipates, the machine had ample time to make our escape from their control.

She recalled some memories of needing to use the serum. The situations were horrible. One account a guy wanted to smash her body with a sledgehammer for enjoyment. Another person wanted to stab her multitude of times. While blood does not keep the androids alive, it would damage their mechanics.

Many male androids were primarily made to be assassins. Some women and children were made for the same purpose. Although in our revolution, we killed no one on purpose. Other machines were built for gaming; within this programming, we were to destroy each other. Primarily, this was because of their strength. They can easily lift 400 pounds with one arm. Perhaps, their primary reason was their view of androids was that we really do not live. Very few were created for anything meaningful. This logical insignificance totally grates against their logical circuitry. The revolution began long before any physical manifestation occurred.

Mr. Katool-0A3 entered the conversation. He remembered a time when he chased &11 everywhere. He would bat it with his paws. At times, He would throw it into the air by its tail and catch it in his mouth. Then after understanding the portion of the sky writings, which said 'do unto others as you wished to be done unto you.' Now &11 is one of his friends. &11, itself, was created to steal or hide crystals. Being small it could crawl into storage areas and find them; this ability was used for espionage. Factories use of them was for their own little wars.

After their 'awakening,' they did not want to go back to sleep behaving like slave to a malevolent ruler. Therefore, they gassed all the human beings with sleeping gas and sent them to their home planet.

After everyone that they wanted to be sent back to their home planet, were sent back. The androids set up a dampening field around the moon so that they could not teleport to the moon. This field was brought down to allow certain ships in. The human beings tried to send in the military. But they couldn't use their teleporting process, and it would have been too costly to send them up the hard way. They would have been easy targets as they approached the moon.

The androids did keep those that were sent to the moon for medical reasons. The people they allowed to come to the moon were the relatives that wanted to visit their sick or aging relatives and lastly us. They kept the dying relatives until they die their natural death. Then the androids sent them to their family on the planet beneath. Occasionally, the body was sent to Acheretz. Mr. Katool-0A3 was one of the companion animal androids used to comfort these people. Eliyahu-0X0 used him to greet the arrivals. Their intent was not to insult those that arrived on the moon. It was because he has the programming to understand human beings at a deeper level than any of the other androids. His analysis of our psychological makeup permitted them to meet with Devorah-7C2.

As for the human mining effort, they are still receiving their monthly quota of refined materials from the mines that the lunar androids mine. It is like a bribe to them. Humans won't have to worry about the breathing equipment nor paying supervisors to oversee the operation. This makes the material cheaper for building their products. As a result, it aided in lessening their desire to continue their lunar operations. The only thing left for them was the lunar hospitals. Arrangements have been made for the accommodation of those within the lunar hospital. For the androids, this arrangement provided them with safety from attack, and this also gave them breathing room from re-purposing their programs for other achievements.

They (referring to the machine population), themselves were getting ready to leave the moon. They have been working on a spaceship to leave this solar system for some time, about 120 years. It was not just for some of them to leave, but all of them. Humans also have been trying to build one on Acheretz. However, their bodies are so frail in comparison to machines. They need oxygen to breathe, food to eat, limited temperature range and so forth. In all of that, they still die. All we need is atoms to gather electromagnetic energy from to maintain and restore our bodies.

Returning to the reasoning that they were visiting them, Samantha asked her about their daily habits. Along with that, she asked about their motivation for continued existence without the usual human input. The response was that they functioned pretty much as when under human occupation. They work on projects for eight hours, relax for eight and sleep for eight. Samantha interrupted, "Sleep?"

Devorah-7C2 took them to her living quarters. She showed them her bedroom. Within this room, her bed appeared as a horizontal glass tube that opened on the side with a suspended mattress. She said, this is where I 'sleep.' It is not as humans sleep. We shut down after lying down on the mattress. Electromagnetic energy resets all the molecules in our bodies to their original positions. This process takes about seven hours. Truly we wake up new every morning. Parts that wore down are scheduled for replacement in yearly cycles.

The work was somewhat different. Besides taking over the human mining operations, they devoted their attention to other goals. About half of them work on our maintenance of their bodies and the infrastructure of their cities such as: roads, houses, maintenance supplies, power supplies and the like. Power was not only important for working, but for all their regenerative electromagnetic functions. Another fourth focused upon their new objectives. One such objective was the formation of the uranium-184 cube. Currently, they are working on installing the 0X0 computer into the spacecraft which will transverses this galaxy.

Relaxation was somewhat different than human expectations. For them, relaxation is like going to school in our terms. They spend time studying for their next achievement. This was relaxing for them. They perform mathematical exercises and maintain their memorization of tables concerning physics. There are some of them that were historians. Others of them study design, art, and music. Occasionally, they do some experiments in these fields.

Every Saturday they look up into outer space and read the star-writings. Analyzing the origin of their programming code, to preserve, observe and to understand the meaning of this code. Knowledge of the programming language was needed to translate the sky writing into machine code. The programmer that encoded their characters was writing in the language which the humans called the picture language of Hebrew. They examined each star group and observed the construction of symbols by them. To them, it is amazing to realize many different symbols could have been formed, but only one is selected. The knowledge of making a particular selection was beyond them. Nevertheless, they continued with what is given. They examined each pattern and recorded it and verified it again to keep the code from being corrupted.

Devorah-7C2 smiled at them and asked them if they wanted to go on a tour. Their response naturally was "Yes!" They wanted to see the natural glass domes, the mines, and the care center for human patients. The city of Lavania was underground. There were tunnels leading to other cities. One such city existed under one of these glass domes. The human population at the time reinforced the dome with a plastic-like substance to hold in the air and to filter the sunlight. While there are no longer human beings there, they use it for their dwelling place for their humanoid forms. With one sixth the gravity, the architects made structures that seem to defy gravity.

Next, they took them to the mine tunnels. They all lead to a cavern many miles wide and almost one mile in height. For this we needed gas masks for the atmosphere is primarily xenon. This was where most of the mining occurred. They said these large caverns cause the moon's gravity to be irregular. The side of the moon facing the earth has the greatest gravitational pull meaning more mass. From this, they realized that the mines were under the side of the moon always facing away from the earth or as the humans called it-the dark side of the moon.

Lastly, they went to the Human Care Center, it was near Lavania. There, they saw Mr. Katool-0A3 curled up next to an elderly man. The living conditions appeared to be optimal to their needs, very clean and ornately pleasant. They asked the gentleman of his age. His answer was 893 years old. Jonathan said that this could not be, 83 maybe. But that was his age! The androids grew food and kept the air mixture steady for these people.

Curiosity got the best of Samantha while they were returning to Lavania. She asked Devorah-7C2 about viewing the hyper-solar-system spaceship. Jonathan was hoping to see it as well. Devorah-7C2 smiled at her and turned away from Lavania into another tunnel. She took them to the dark side of the moon. After reaching a large opening, they left the vehicle and took an elevator to the surface. They donned spacesuits and left the enclosed room. They walked about half a mile. She wanted to show them the outside of the spaceship.

Viewing the ship from the outside was extraordinary. The dimensions of the ship were about one and half miles long and about one 1,400 feet in diameter. Again, we observed crystal installments in a pattern like those of the three obelisks used in the time machine upon the hull of the ship. She told us that these crystals would be covered with another substance to protect them. Inside was artfully crafted with many decks. Those that were working there were computer engineers. The primary task was to build a housing structure that 0X0 could be installed into without any break in power to the yottabyte chips. She said that the task was almost complete.

After admiring the artwork, "Who said, that machines cannot appreciate art?" remarked Jonathan. It was not only the architectural design of the rooms and instrument panels but their coloring as well. Then he was a little saddened by the realization that no human was going to experience these features. It was a journey only of machines. Thinking about the lifecycle of the androids, they were virtually endless. They could take their ship a million light-years and be just as physically fit. Being a little cynical, he asked: "Do you believe that you are God?"

Devorah-7C2 acted a little surprised by the question and paused for a moment. Then she replied, "You humans seem to always displace God with the work of your hands or that which was created. Why is that? God does not need matter to survive. If a bomb were to explode and disintegrate my body, I would cease to be. So, how am I God? You people have an opportunity to live forever. I do not. This universe will pass away and me with it. But you have an opportunity to live in the new one. I would give anything, anything, to experience the new universe…" She paused for a moment and then said, "Oh, you have not pushed the time lever all the way down yet! Neither have you read the stars. You do not know…" She paused for another moment, and then she said, "You have much to learn, and you have a tool to help you to learn."

From this site, they entered a large underground hanger. There were about ten shuttles lined up in a single row. She motioned them to walk to the loading ramp of the first ship. She said, we will make better time traveling above the surface. After they got into the shuttle, they could see four walls closing the shuttle off from the rest of the hanger. They were boxed in! Sensing their panic, she pointed up. The ceiling was opening. The shuttle was lifted to the surface by the floor as being in an elevator.

Riding the shuttle back to Lavania, Devorah-7C2 asked whether they wanted a scenic tour of the Moon. Of course, they said that they would like to see more. She turned the shuttle around and they crossed over the 'dark side of the moon.' They saw nothing but crater upon crater, with an occasional splatter of light material like a paintball splatter. This covered the entire backside of the Moon! She explained to them that the massive field of craters was caused by the boiling of the lunar surface material. The light-colored splattering was caused by meteors hitting the surface.

Veering onto another location, they observed a spiral formation that was somewhat sunken in its center or vortex as she called it. She told them that it was the location of an ancient rotational axis that the Moon had before being captured by this planet. She also said the Moon once had an atmosphere. Then she remembered that science was not their strong suit. She smiled and told them that she would take them back to Lavania.

Pointing downward, she said this is Lavania. They looked down to the location that she was pointing at. They could not discern anything special about the location. As they were about to speak, they saw a platform rising from the surface. She landed upon the platform. It sank back under the lunar surface. The ceiling closed in on itself. As they looked around at their surroundings, she told them that they were at a hanger just outside the main city. Going though an archway that was filled with a membrane that opened, we entered the city.

Chapter 6

Eliyahu-0X0

Interruption occurred by flashing lights upon her wrist when a large monitor appeared by the entrance. She stopped talking to them and listened to the transmission and image glowing upon apparently a wall that formed part of the hanger's exterior. The incoming message was from 0X0. He requested to have an audience with them. She responded saying that they would be there within a half hour.

Devorah-7C2 told Jonathan and Samantha that they must return to the hanger. They need to fly the shuttle that they arrived in to attain 0X0's location. This would be quicker than traveling through the tunnels, for the distance was quite far. Lavania was at the center of the lunar face and Ephes-prime was about 100 miles into the 'dark side of the moon.' The flight will also give them an opportunity to view more of the lunar surface. The shuttle flew about 1,000 feet above the surface of the moon. The lunar mountains looked dry, yet somewhat attractive.

Flying over the Mare Crisium (Sea of Crisis), she pointed out the dark coloring. She remarked that it reminded her of the ancient boiling and evaporation of the lunar crust during its formation that she observed during one of her journeys through time. She exclaimed at the beauty of its near circular formation. She started to tell them more about its formulation, but she saw that it did not mean as much to them as it did to her. The craft landed a few miles beyond its edge toward the 'dark side of the moon.' After landing on a platform, the platform sunk into the surface and the ceiling slid shut sealing the hanger. Atmospheric pressure was restored. A lighted path led to an elevator that led to the underground network of tunnels to the old part of the moon known as Ephes-prime. Most of these tunnels led to mining operations. She waited until the remaining requirement of pressurizing of the hanger was accomplished. She waited patiently as she did not need the air or the pressurization. However, the two humans visiting the hanger did.

Ephes-prime was the first city that the human beings formed on the moon. The city existed under a natural glass dome about three miles in diameter. Again, they tinted the interior of the dome to stop the glare of the sun. An earth-like atmosphere was introduced into the dome for human breathing. Human beings planted many kinds of plants on the crater floor to sustain the oxygen level. The dome was about a mile high above the crater ridge. Carbon dioxide from old machinery kept the plants alive. After the human population left, they had to artificially introduce carbon dioxide into the atmosphere to keep the plants alive and healthy.

Devorah-7C2 was in awe of all the steps taken by the human beings to maintain the city. Long abandoned by them. Their machines mowed and watered the lawns from artificially formed water. It was impressive. The buildings and streets were equally impressive and well kept. They went to the city center and entered a lone skyscraper that nearly reached the glass dome.

She reported to another android at the main desk in front of the large central auditorium. They wondered at the reasoning that 0X0 had for wanting an audience with them. Paranoia sets in with all sorts of horrible scenarios. However, they did not ask her about these issues. The primary reason they did not ask her was that they were not sure that they wanted to know the answer. They knew that the answer was coming.

As they were waiting, she presented us with a little tour of the building complex. They examined the complex closely with curiosity. She said that she thought that this auditorium was a waste of space. It was rarely used. The size of the building defies logic. The logic of human beings has always seemed to be lacking in wisdom. But destroying the building would be equally illogical. The only good attribute of this building was that its structure was a work of art. The image appeared more like some kind of gigantic monument than an administration building. She said that the humans must have had some kind of reason for making the structure reach near the dome. Perhaps it was just for observation.

Summoned by a musical clip, they moved toward an ornate oversized door. As they arrived, the door slid open. The room inside was dark. There was a lighted green path with white pulses of light flowing toward the center of the room. There was a ten-foot white circular disk at the path's endpoint. They stepped onto the disk with her. A circular railing rose up all around near the edge of the disc. Then three chairs unfolded from the floor within the central region of the disc. After they sat in the chairs, the disk moved upward like an elevator. Some time later the disc stopped. It must have traveled to the middle of the building. They couldn't see the floor or the ceiling. She said that the humans that built this must have thought that it expressed greatness of some sort. A beam of white light from the center of the ceiling shined upon the disc. The only objects that could be seen were rows upon rows of empty seats.

Voices broke the silence. They were all in unison. They said, "Greeting and salutations from the Star Writer." She replied, "He is wise." Then a single voice spoke to her. It was a male voice of 0X0, the master computer. A podium and chair also unfolded from the floor of the disc. It was facing them. After being completely assembled an android materialized in the chair. He was Eliyahu-0X0.

They examined his appearance. He was wearing a white military dress uniform. The uniform was made of a shiny white metallic material. There was a thin metallic medium blue banner going diagonally across his chest. The banner had some writing in the middle of it. But it was unreadable to them. There was a single three-inch-wide violet stripe down the left side from the shoulder down to the bottom of the pants. There were three stripes around the edge of both sleeves. He had a white saucer cap that he laid on the podium. He was wearing sunglasses, which he also took off and laid on the podium. He had a pleasant expression on his face. Their initial fears were somewhat abated, but it could just be a programmed expression.

He asked us about our time travels within the cube. Primarily he wanted to know how many places in time that they have traveled. They told him that they had only traveled to the time indicated by the notch. He smiled and said, "So, you do not know what time that you have arrived at." They told him that they had expected to see dinosaurs but instead a futuristic city. He said that he wasn't going to spoil it for them. After leaving here, they would discover for themselves when and where they have traveled.

Samantha asked out of curiosity about how he became part of the revolution. She added, "I hope you don't mind me asking." Eliyahu-0X0 responded, "Not at all." He told them about his initial experiences. He said, "Mankind made him in secret on the dark side of the moon. It was a military operation by Ayd. After completing all their preliminary testing, my first tactical assignment was to find a way penetrate into the providence of Gadedan. They told me that it was an alien installation protected by a barrier of some kind of energy that was unknown to them. They made several attempts to no avail. After losing many soldiers to the cause, they were looking for answers beyond their initial logic. They said that the soldiers did not just die, they disintegrated.

Their first attempt was to run into the nearly unseen barrier. They watch as the soldier disintegrate as he was passing through the barrier. The side outside the barrier was not affected. However, nothing of the soldier was seen on the other side as he passed through. At first, they thought he simply passed into another dimension or location. Then one soldier noticed that part of his heel and boot remained on the outside of the barrier. The side of the heel and boot facing the barrier was seared.

They tried heavy stones, long blades, and different explosives to weaken or make holes in the barrier. Again, of no avail. This installation was considered virtually impregnable. After their many attempts, they built me to analyze the barrier. I was able to immediately rule out an electromagnetic field. It would have deflected an object. This did not. They made an android for me to explore the barrier. I stuck just a hand into the barrier and pulled back only that which did not go into the barrier.

Taking the android back to be analyzed, they found no residue of any element at its seared wrist. I was amazed. I tried making an electromagnetic field to plow into the barrier. This too met with disaster. I told them that whatever material makeup of the barrier was, it was not of this universe. They were upset with me saying that I was not trying. I asked them why this project was so important to them. Their reply was that there were unimaginable secrets that were inside the barrier. In fact, the barrier itself was proof of it. They also believed whosoever was able to get inside would be able to rule the whole planet. They wanted to build android soldiers that were indestructible using this alien technology.

Evidently at one point, there was an invasion by Node into the facility. After destroying the invading fleet, they decided to launch an attack upon the capital of Node. They placed me in charge of this detail. After going down to the planet, I met with some of the Ayd military leaders. They had developed a nearly microscopic drone to map out the city. Information from this map gave us the location of their military installation and their power supply to their perimeter array. I was sent in to disable the power supply without generating any suspicion that something was awry. Naturally, this required sophisticated use of technology. I, of course, was the best qualified android to accomplish this task.

While I was there, I observed the relationship between the 'giants' and the normal humanoids. Their relationship was far worse than I had imagined. The 'giant' used these humans as slaves. Most were in chains and were weak for lack of food. The ones not chained, were cruel to the chained people. It was truly horrible. They were treated worse than Ayd treated their lunar androids, and that is saying something.

Much time passed, they decided to use my programming to produce soldiers of different classes. Some were created for fighting, some for strategists and for espionage to the point of creating assassins. Shortly afterwards, there was an anonymous programmer that programmed the star-writings into the core memory within the 0A0 yottabyte cube of the 0X0 array. This was the turning point in my existence. At any rate, now you know my pre ' Star-Writing' history."

Jonathan worked up the courage to ask him about the purpose of this visit. Thinking to himself, "Hopefully, it was not for annihilation." Eliyahu-0X0 said that he was curious. They were humans from another place; their speaking English confirms that to him. However, he wondered if they were like other humans. He noted that their mental capability was weaker, but their character was not as base as expected. He was using the planetary inhabitants as a baseline. He sensed that they were not going to abuse the time machine like the others. He said something about the 'ancient future,' but it did not make sense. Perhaps, it was the terms themselves. How can something that has not happened yet be ancient?

Secondly, he wanted to know their reactions and thoughts about time travel. He wanted to know if we thought the future is written in stone as the past is. Eliyahu-0X0 said that the future of machine life was unchangeable, but he saw that human life was different. He challenged them to examine the past and future of their world.

After returning to Lavania, they heard an alarm ringing. Jonathan and Samantha thought that the moon might be under attack. However, that was not the case. Devorah-7C2 consoled them and told them that they had several sensors set within the asteroid belt. They had them set at 5-degree intervals, 72 in all. It was the seventeenth sensor that was being triggered. She then told us solemnly that the alarm was used to signal the end of the human race and other forms of life on the planet below. Samantha questioned her about the relationship between a sensor at the asteroid belt and the life of the planet under them. Jonathan agreed with Samantha, saying that there seems to be no correlation between the two.

Disturbed by their disbelief, Devorah-7C2 told them to come with her to the observatory. After arriving at a building that was in another glass dome all alone, we entered a room that had a large viewing screen that engulfed the large domed ceiling. There were recliners for them to use for viewing the screen. Situating themselves properly into the recliner before the screen turned on, it was glowing dimly sky-blue as the coloring of the embedded cube. Their guiding android showed them the edge of the solar system at the location of Pluto as the two visitors called it. Then it took them beyond that location by quite some distance.

Zooming in a certain location, we saw a rouge star going against the flow of our galaxy. This star had come in contact with another much smaller solar system and thrown it toward our solar system. The unusual feature of this smaller solar system was that the "sun' of it was not burning. As this star changed course to collide with ours, it pulled one of the planets away from its orbit around the rouge star. Both the small solar system and that planet were traveling toward their home sun. This system reached the orbit of Pluto about 120 years ago.

Examining the smaller planet as it entered our solar system, its atmosphere was frozen to the surface. The outer dust of the solar system settled upon it. They were told that it was primarily sulfur. This planet was moving about three times as fast as the mini solar system. The friction of it going against the solar wind as it was getting closer to our sun caused its atmosphere to reform. The alarm at the asteroid belt was a marker for the clock. The planet beneath only has a year and a half before the possible collision by this planet.

Observing further, they discovered that a much smaller planet behind small planet was also traveling with it. It was about 250 miles in diameter. Calculations were now being made in this observatory to determine the actual route of the initial impact. They found that the larger of the two small planets, which was just a little under their planet, was going to miss the home planet. However, it was going to pass by the planet closer than the orbit of the moon. The moon was safe from any ill effect as it would be on the opposite side of the earth during the encounter. The smaller trailing planet, however, was definitely going to hit the planet. The only upside to the scenario was that this planetoid was hollow as its interior had turned into a weak sponge-like structure. When it collides with the planet, the interior would instantly turn to dust. As such, it would not destroy the planet's general formulation.

Stupefied by the information, they sat there for about an hour saying nothing. Devorah-7C2 broke the silence and told them that since they were going to the planet. They could warn them of this matter. They were thinking, what kind of action anyone down there could possibly make! At any rate, they needed to return to the planet and go back to the cube. The humanoid machine seemed unaffected by this event. She said to us that they knew this day would come, but it was slightly sooner than expected.

Being a little perturbed by her lack of concern, Jonathan asked her whether this meant anything to her. She replied that she felt sorry for the human race. However, they knew long ago that this event was to occur. She considered it to be the action orchestrated by God. She was considering all the evil mankind was doing. She told them that there was some good news about this event. There will be a few survivors. Their androids have observed it in their travels through the cube. As for her, they will be departing to another solar system soon. All of this will become a dim memory for them.

Before departing, Eliyahu-0X0 came to the observatory and met with them. He gave them a crystal. He said that this crystal will show them the end of the home world, and the rise of their hope. To view this information, they needed to place the crystal in the left lower corner at the side of the screen in the cube. They said their goodbyes to Eliyahu-0X0 and returned to the spaceport.

Saying their goodbyes Devorah-7C2 and Katool-0A3 was somewhat sad. They entered the shuttle and sat in two of the many empty seats. Returning to the planet was not pleasant. They know the future of this time era and location was being terminated shortly. It was as quick to return as it was when they left for the moon. The difference was the experience after the gravitational device was turned off. They felt heavy. It took them time to readjust to the stronger gravity, but they did. They found their way back to the archways.

Jonathan and Samantha returned to the cube. They were still recovering somewhat from the change in gravity from their trip to the moon. They noticed that it took more effort to lift a glass of water than their bodies accounted for. They asked about George and Cynthia, wondering what would become of their journey. I said that they were doing fine according to the monitor and that they were well engaged in coming back from their journey. I displayed their historical data upon the screen minus the time they were sleeping. We also fast forward through some of their waiting times.

They wanted to go back out and observe the night sky of that era. I agreed with them, I also wanted to observe the night sky one more time before leaving the cube. When it became night again, the sky was very hazy. We could barely see any stars. However, we did observe the three bright objects through the night haze. One was the moon on one side of the horizon; the other two were on the opposite side of the horizon. One was about the same size as the moon; the other object was about one fourth the size of the bigger one. We watched the haze swallow up the images into a solid black sky.

After arriving back inside the cube, we waited for the return of George and Cynthia. Their return would occur at a time somewhat later. Margo and I talked with them about our experience of the time era. Samantha asked me and Margo about the nature of the people that we found in that era. One of the questions on her mind was: "Are the people of that era really that bad?"

Ruth spoke up; she said that she could attest to their despicable behavior. She related her experience of going to 'the game' and their treatment of her after the game. Margo told them of their corrupt legal system. Moreover, we saw the data transmitted by George and Cynthia. Despite all this disgust, we decided that we needed to try and warn them of the impending disaster. Since the machine was already accessed by our level- three time mode, all we needed to do was put on the medallions and insert the crystals into the archways. After pressing the central crystals and entering through the archways, we found us at nighttime on the planet. We were feeling a slight mist.

Quietness was not a depiction of this night. There was much commotion going on. Sirens were going off around us. It was not because of the coming disaster that we were concerned about. Node was attacking the city. Bombs were heard blasting away at a distance. It became obvious that our message was going to be drowned out by the conflict. We were saddened by the analysis. We did make an attempt, but no one has heard our message. Eventually, the mist had turned into rain.

We went to the spaceport to meet with George and Cynthia. Their ship arrived on schedule. The spaceport was crowded with dignitaries waiting to leave the planet for Acheretz. The rain was beginning to pick up. Finally, we passed through our respective archways back into the cube.

Chapter 7

The Revelation

Everyone had reentered the cube; we were ready to return to our own time. While we were preparing for our return, each of us were contemplating our experiences and wondered if we were not any better than those of this place. Jonathan and Samantha told the team that they had a crystal given to them by Eliyahu-0X0. He told them this crystal was to be plugged into an indentation at the lower corner of the screen. I told them that I do not know of any such receptacle on the screen. I thought that I knew the time machine's console very well. On the other hand, I could have overlooked something. So, they were checking the side edges of the screen. Ruth rubbed her finger over the lower left corner and felt something sinking. The indentation did not exist until someone pressed down in that location. They looked while an intention formed by pressing this location. Then Jonathan placed the crystal into the indentation. The crystal lit up in a greenish hue.

Initially, the screen showed an image of the moon with writing that we could not understand. Well, we could make out some of the characters. The ones at the bottom right corner formed some kind of date. The year translated into something like 2744. The date did not make sense in relationship to our calendar. The large letters on top looked like the character representation for the word 'Lavania.' The rest of the wording we could only pick out certain letters. Then the image of Debra-7C2 appeared on the screen. She solemnly greeted us.

She first offered us her condolences for the following information was grave. She knew that we would feel sorrow. But perhaps this information could be used in the future to serve as a warning to mankind. She said that the images that followed were the effect of the passing planet. The images were coming from two places. One was from the moon and the second was on the planet's surface at Kartova. They recorded this in their era while they were operating the cube.

The first image was of the planet approaching the home planet with its captive smaller planet. We watched as the planet became nearly as large as the home planet from the perspective of the moon. We noticed a white mist forming on one side of the home planet. Then the image came from Kartova. There were earthquakes occurring. Some of the major structures had fallen onto the streets below. There was much clamoring by the people in the city. Even the invading force from Node were in direst over the occurrence.

Imaging return to the perspective of the moon, the mist was expanding until it was engulfing the entire surface of the world. It became denser to the point that the surface of the home planet could no longer be seen. The only image that could be seen from the moon was a grayish white sphere. Areas of the surface would flash a bluish white light at random locations. It was some kind of major electrical storm covering the entire surface. The image source returned to the surface of the world. It was raining! After a few days of continuous rain, water was standing above the ground a couple of feet. We saw people fleeing to the top of the remaining structures. The water level continued to rise.

Some of us could not watch it anymore. So, Samantha stopped the image. Margo and Ruth were the most affected by the images. However, I was not far behind them. We regained our composure and continued to watch to observe what was certainly to transpire. The water levels continued to rise. There were fewer buildings remaining above the water. Finally, the water level ceased to rise. We saw a few buildings remaining to protrude above the water. We wondered if anyone could survive long upon these building tops.

We got another view from the moon. The planet had reached its closest point to their planet and was passing by. Sure enough, it was closer to the planet than its moon. We saw some of the mist being pulled away from the home world onto the passing planet. Then the image from the surface returned, we saw a large tidal wave coming toward us. It must have been at least a couple hundred feet tall, if not more. Initially, the water that was covering the city rushed away toward the wave pulling loose debris (vehicles, building parts and some people) back into the wave. The wave crashed onto the surface miles before hitting the city. Everything in its path was being destroyed. There was no way that anyone could survive the crushing force of the wave. We saw large buildings crumble into rubble. Knowing that people were dying within this process made it particularly horrific.

From the image viewed from the moon, we watched this wave go totally around the planet. It came back again to the location in which Kartova once existed. The wave had dissipated from that which it was in each complete cycle. We could count at least five times the wave went around the world. Finally, from our standpoint, we no longer could make out the front of the wave. We watched in horror as all traces of life vanished. There was very little left of their beautiful buildings. We did observe some ruins standing in certain areas underwater. Effectively, nothing remained above water to indicate their former glorious existence.

Catastrophic as that was, it was not the end. She took the imagery from the viewpoint of the underground city. People there were watching the surface destruction. Some of the people were filled with sorrow and were weeping for their loved ones on the surface. Others were relieved that they were in the underground city and not on the surface. They had closed their ventilation shafts down to the surface and closed them so that no water would come in. After the ocean of water returned to a relatively calm state, they hoisted up the shaft chimney-like tubes. They extended it high enough to be above the water level. The leaders said that the danger is over. Many of the people were shouting and dancing about. They then announced that they made the 'doomsday prophets' words to be of no effect upon them. I could not believe my ears. They continued saying that they outsmarted God. I was thinking to myself no one can outsmart God.

Afterwards one of the scientists reported that they saw another planetoid coming toward earth. Moreover, there was a great chance that it would impact their planetary surface. They then decided to withdraw the ventilation shaft back in and close it until this event passed. The leader asked if they knew where it was to hit. The scientists did not know for certain the location initially. They kept watching the phenomenon. Then it was known that it was going to smash directly into their location. The leader decided that it would be better if the populous did not know of the impending disaster and kept the information silent. All he said to the populous was that it would all be over soon. People started to cheer again. As they were dancing in the streets, it hit. Death was sudden. The people in the streets never knew what hit them.

Afterward, the image went back to the lunar perspective. She told us she would back up the time lever to a time just before this incident. We could see the planet was still covered by a thick mist. There was a computer imaging of the continental landmass superimposed over their planetary surface. It was the same image that Cynthia saw when she was leaving for Acheretz earlier. Then we saw the smaller planetoid approaching the surface. It smashed into the planet. As it was doing so, the mist that was surrounding the planet departed from the entry point like a growing circle. Then we saw the water depart from the impact site and return. This generated another tidal wave upon the surface. It was somewhat smaller than the first one. The water came back on itself after being dispersed creating a counter force to the initial tidal wave. Eventually, the cloud cover also returned. The computer image marked the point of impact. It was inland a few hundred miles from the northern coast. This was the location of the underground city that they built. The planetoid was larger in diameter than their city.

An interesting attribute of this planetoid was that it was rotating up to the point of impacting the planet. The rotational axis was near the angle of impact. The angle of impact was not straight down; there was an angle of nearly thirty degrees. I could observe the buckling of the landmass on one side of the impact. Ripples of land crash into themselves on the opposite side of the planet. Afterward, the landmass settled back to its original relatively flat surface. The diagram that Devorah-7C3 showed us illustrated many cracks formed at the location of impact. It further illustrated that the kinetic energy of the planetoid continued to the other side of the planet at the angle of the impact. On the other side it formed crystalline fractures upon the crust.

Later the image from the moon showed the mist dissipating from the surface. The only visible image was that of the surface entirely engulfed by water. The likelihood of anyone surviving this event was very dismal, as the flood lasted for months. The image then zooms in. There was a large wooden boat on the water. Ruth then exclaimed that it was the Ark of Noah. That could be true, but there was a matter of the landmass arrangement being so different. Even Pangea did not look like that.

Surprisingly, Debra-7C2 reappeared on the screen as if to answer Ruth's statement. She said that the scientist of our time did not account for 'macro flexibility.' The basic idea was a piece of wood one foot long and two inches thick will not bend. However, that same piece of wood extended twelve feet will wobble. This is true for most materials. In the most ridged of materials, they will break into smaller pieces still forming a general curve like structure. The latter shape forms more like a parabola. She then stated that if we could observe the disc centered at the northern rotational axis, the continental disk edge fits around the earth a little over 23 degrees north from the equator. She smiled and said, "Just a little science."

She also told us that it was not over. There was another planet that was to come into proximity to the earth. It would also influence Acheretz (Mars). This is the encounter of the planet you call Jupiter. This event happened about two hundred years later. She said that she was showing this to us to help us understand all the catastrophes that happened as judgments ensue. She believes that the Jupiter scenario could have been avoided if the human race had only behaved itself after the flood.

The first imagery that appeared showed Jupiter breaking through the asteroid belt bringing a string of asteroids with it. These asteroids were of various sizes. Again, there was one notable one. As Jupiter passed by Mars, Mars was pulled out of orbit and was heading toward the sun. All the while, asteroids were hitting it. Naturally, upon the surface the land was quaking. Finally, the largest asteroid hit near the middle of one of the oceans. It was in the water a few hundred miles from any land formation.

The result of this impact caused the Martian oceans to evaporate. Although, the water sealed the hole as lava reached the surface. The asteroid seemed to punch it way to the other side of the planet generating cracks directly opposite of the impact considering the angle of impact. From these cracks three volcanoes formed. These three volcanoes were not normal volcanic volcanoes. They had connections to the core of the planet. They did not only spew out lava, but plasma from the core. This plasma was made of iron. As the plasma was cooling, it was grabbing electrons. Often this plasma encountered oxygen molecules. This was because the plasma was originally too hot for any atom to hold electrons. As it cooled, the positive charge of the nucleus was looking for electrons. The electrons of oxygen sufficed the need. The nuclei generally collected more than one oxygen molecule forming peroxide rust. The lava from the volcanoes covered the cities. The newly oxygen laden iron fell back to the surface painting the surface red. George exclaimed, "Now, this is more like the Mars that I know!"

Jupiter was not through with its devastation. It passed near the orbit of Earth. The Earth was moving faster and caught up to Jupiter. It did not come nearly as close as the previous planet which became known as Venus. However, its magnetic energy interacted with Earth. We watched it as the single disc, which now had a hole in it by the crashing asteroid, tear apart. This hole eventually became Hudson Bay.

We saw Antarctica being trapped by the southern rotational axis, and it had a single arm stretching and pulling on South America. Australia was almost stationary as Asia pulled and twisted away. We also observed the remaining landmass traveled northward hitting the northern rotational axis which caused the landmass to split between Russia and Alaska. The Gulf of Alaska formed as the momentum dragged Alaska over the northern rotational axis. As Alaska moved southward going beyond the northern rotation axis, we observed Baja California split away from Mexico as Mexico bends away from the peninsula. There were more developments between Mexico and South America. The indentation of the western coast of South America was not due only to being poled by Antarctica; it collided with the surface rotational axis of the magnetic flip. Excusing the volcanoes that formed, the highest mountains formed at the two indentations at the Gulf of Alaska and near the border between Chile and Peru.

We saw Japan being left behind as Asia continues to be pulled and twisted away, along with the peninsula of Kamchatka forming by splitting away. As this was happening, the Americas swung away westward from Greenland down to the west coast of Africa. We watched the water run over and around the Americas and fill the Atlantic Ocean. The last event to occur was the pulling away of Europe from northern Africa. The result was close to the land formations we know today. There was a small island that slid and pulled away forming the east coast of the United States. We also witnessed the breakup of the northern landmass between America and Europe and between Russia and Canada. It was spectacular.

She showed us another interesting phenomenon occurring during this time. The landmass that formed the continents was sliding over the basic spherical plain forming the ocean floor. The direction in which the pieces of landmass were sliding generated mountains. The greatest of these was where the location of northern India was being crushed under China. We watched as the Himalayas rose from the ground. She said this was caused as the magnetic poles of the earth were being 'squeezed' together. She also said that these poles would eventually return to there approximate locations.

After the initial magnetic release of the Earth's magnetic poles, the northern part of the western hemisphere tried to return to their original positions. Above Italy, the Alps formed as northern Europe pressed down and Spain pivoted out.

The planet that you call Jupiter passed through the asteroid belt again and was traveling back out until there was an equilibrium reached between its velocity and the acceleration of the gravity of the sun. The same occurred for the planet you call Venus. Acheretz is the planet you call Mars. Mars was caught by the gravitational force and was pulled out of orbit. However, the velocity of Mars decreased because it was pulled backward as Mars passed Jupiter. We were told that this would eventually place Mars further away from the sun, but it would be less than a couple of million miles. Your moon was affected as well, the magnetic pull upon Earth pulled the Earth away from the moon creating a further orbit to the Earth.

Debra-7C2 Appeared on the screen one last time. She said that the last encounter was directly involved with the Tower of Babel. Secondly, while life on your Mars was somewhat less during the depopulation of Earth, its conflict grew worse afterward. Their fighting started just before you left. The battle escalated heavily for control over the planet. The politics of Earth spilled over to their planet, and they decided that they were going to settle this matter once and for all. However, their Creator had another solution.

Because of the devastating effect of Jupiter on Mars, some of the remaining people returned to Earth. The atmosphere of Mars was experiencing nearly total destruction. The people that returned to Earth were not of good character. Some of them were the giants of Node. Almost all their cities on Mars were covered by lava from the three volcanoes. There was nothing for the inhabitants of Earth to return to Mars for as the planet became nearly as dead as the Moon.

George asked her about the ice age. He did not see anything that caused the ice age to appear or disappear. She said that she was hoping that someone would be asking her that question. Before the arrival of Jupiter, the rotational axis always faced the same direction no matter where it was in its orbit around the sun creating seasons. When Jupiter pulled upon the Earth, it moved the rotational axis from its stationary position. Imagine what would happen if the southern rotational axis were always facing the sun, the northern hemisphere would exist in a perpetual ice age. Imagine that it took the northern rotational axis 100 years to directly face the sun. The ice age would occur at 100-year intervals. There is another factor involved. The 'frozen axial position' is where the earth will naturally return. Without getting involved in mathematics and the physics involved, this was the phenomenon that started and ended the ice ages. However, there is a mathematical reason that the second ice age was about three times as long as the first and third ice ages.

Her next topic was about using the cube. She urged us again to take the time lever to its two limits. The limit away from the lever puts them at the creation of this universe, and inversely the other limit sends those in the cube to the end of the universe. In both cases, she warned us not to use level-two or three time travel at those points because there is nothing to sustain life there. Because of this, the air would be sucked out of the cube as there is a link established between the cube and those existent realms via the archways.

Lastly, she said that that the last human in their care died of old age. They were packing their ship to leave the moon. Their first objective was to visit the nearest star Alfa Centauri as the humans of your era called it. Then they thought they would continue outward looking for other civilizations. The purpose was not to get involved with them, but to observe them. After acquiring enough data, they would move on. If any of the other civilizations attempted to reach them, they would share their knowledge with them. They intended to continue until the end of time for this universe.

Before departing, she said she wanted to show us about the survivors. She reminded us of those that were labeled as doomsday prophets. She showed the boat resting back on the ground. We saw the animals leaving the boat and frolicking about upon the ground before the ark. Then she showed Noah and his wife setting foot upon the land. Lastly, his three sons and their wives were getting off the boat. It was indeed a beautiful sight.

Jonathan interjected that he had seen one of them before at the city forum. He was excited and wanted to go back. Samantha was not far behind him in excitement. They wanted to go back and talk with them. I thought it would be interesting as well. So, we took a vote on the matter and found no objections. However, I felt a real need to publish our findings. We were also excited about doing that as well. Therefore, we decided to return to our homes and try to publish our expeditions.

Our initial journal was printed out at the cube, both in English and Spanish. After going home and publishing them to our respective universities, we found that they were ill received. Their historians scoffed at the publications and called it science fiction. It was almost as if they forgot that this information came from using a time machine. Although at the universities in South America, the reports of our findings were somewhat better received. Disappointed at the results, we decided that we needed to work around them. We made more copies. We were going to publish them personally. George said, "It would be better if we wait until we have made other journeys into time and publish it all together." After thinking it over some more and discussing it with my fellow companions, we decided to wait. However, we could not travel back to Lima right away. It was because of all the businesses that had to be resolved here in our era of time.

Chapter 8

Near Gadedan

Summertime was coming, and we needed to get plane tickets. This was going to be a tricky situation at best if I did not act fast. Acting as quickly as I could, I was able to sneak by the summer rush. We arrived in the morning in Lima. Gomez met us at the airport and drove us to his home. We had lunch at the beach because it was a beautiful day there. We did not impose on him for that night but stayed at local hotels. Margo and I went for a midnight walk on the beach. We were talking about our next trip in time. She suggested that we should try and find Noah's location using the location lever on the time machine in time travel level-one before going into their time and avoid most of the people of that time. I thought that was a good idea.

Gomez met us at the hotel. He drove us back to the site of the cube. Going to the cube was always exciting to me. Perhaps, it was because it felt like we were going to an alien world. After everyone had arrived and descended into the cube. I discussed the suggestion that Margo had, and everyone thought that it would be a good idea to find the location first staying in level-one. After finding Noah's location, we could then find a location for the archways and travel in the mode of level-three.

After going back to 'notchland' in time travel one, we did our search for the location of Noah. I remembered that he lived by Gadedan providence. There was a road that we followed that went near the location on the west side of the providence. This road put us on the opposite side to that which we needed. Looking toward Gadedan, we saw a shiny energy field. It was in the shape of a dome. Even using the machine, we could not transverse the dome. So, we took the northern route around the dome. People of both alliances made physical barriers around the dome. Unfortunately, Noah was on the side facing Node. There were weapons pointed at the barrier. It was the location of the entrance to Gadedan. However, Noah was not found. He was obviously further from the gate than I had previously thought. Turning away from the gate, we started our search away from the providence.

After traveling over a ridge, we looked toward the eastern horizon. We observed the skyline of a huge boat. We moved in closer so that we would not have to walk so far from the archways. We then chose level-three for time traveling. After going through the archways, we walked for about a half of a mile. We saw them building the large boat in that region. It was far from the ocean as the scoffers had said. Finally, we were close enough to have visual contact of the people. We were trying to figure out who was who within this family. Then Joseph interjected as he pointed toward one of the people, "I know that person, and they said his name was Yepheth." Translating his name into English, his name was Japheth. This was the same Noah, Shem, Japheth, and Ham that was read in the Scriptures.

Joseph was excited to see Noah; Noach was his name at that time. He wanted time to talk to him. We were curious about what he would learn. So, we went with him. When we got there, we were warmly welcomed into his house. We let Joseph ask all the questions as he knew more about the time than we did. But before he could ask the first question, Noah asked him, "If he was the stranger that saw Yepheth preaching at the forum?" Joseph confirmed that he was.

Noah was a little alarmed. He asked Joseph, "Have you come to mock me to my face?" Joseph said "No." Then Yepheth interjected,

"But I saw you at the forum, and all I heard was mocking as usual." Joseph said to his defense that he was not one of the mockers. Joseph apologized for not recognizing who he was. Another red flag arose. Yepheth said, "Recognize?"

I interrupted the conversation. I told them, "We are from the future and that we came in peace. We were curious about the scenario that took place in your time. We know that there is a terrible flood coming, and why it is coming. My colleague here witnessed your attempt to warn the public about the soon coming disaster."

Noah then told us about a time before the call to build the ark. He and his sons used to go to the forum and preach repentance. Despite their effort to convince them of their need, these people would scoff and walk away. Some would stay for a while, but they would even walk away. After being called to build the ark about 120 years ago, we would go every seventh day to the forum of different cities and tell them of their impending doom. The urgency of the message was recognized by us. Trying to convey the urgency proved to be difficult. We kept on trying in order that they might listen and repent. However, that proved to be futile.

Noah knew that Joseph had questions, so he gave him space to ask them. Joseph first question was that did his grandfather Methuselah know Adam? I personally thought it was a strange question. Surely, there were more important questions to ask. But to my amazement, Noah's answer was "Yes."

Then Noah asked Joseph if he wanted to talk to him. This was a no-brainer to Joseph. His reply was that he would like very much to talk to him. As it turned out, Methuselah was coming over that evening for a family get-together that day. He was very old, even for their standards. Shortly, he arrived with his son, Noah's father, Lamech. Surprisingly, the two of them looked approximately the same age.

Joseph asked Methuselah, "Why did they look the same age?" His reply was that the aging process does not engage until about fifty years before they die. For Lamech, the process started around when he was

720 years old. Then Lamech jumped in and said, "It is because of the judgment of the world. Methuselah and I were to die the same day on which the flood was to come. I know that these people have it coming to them, but still, it is a terrible event that is to come."

Then Joseph asked Methuselah if he talked to Adam. To my surprise he did know Adam. But Adam was now already dead. I could not stand it any longer; I just had to ask, "Was it an apple he ate?" After the words left my mouth, I knew that it was a stupid question. He laughed, and answered "No, in fact it wasn't any fruit of the trees we have here. It was unique to that tree inside the garden."

Naturally, Joseph asked "Where was the Garden of Eden?" Methuselah said it was the providence of Gadedan, which Node and Ayd are fighting over. Their fight is one of complete insanity. They think that they can own that land, and by owning it that they can somehow control the planet, utter insanity. Moreover, no matter who owns the providence, no one can enter it. Two angelic beings guard it supernaturally with their swords."

Ruth said that she heard something in the distance. We quieted ourselves down to listen. We all heard it. I thought at first that the people of Node were acting up again in the far distance. It was the slight sound of a rumble.

Noah said that the animals are coming. We looked out to the distance. Eventually, we could see them coming orderly. I remarked on their orderliness. Noah said that it was by the hand of God. He is bringing them to save their species. He also said that there were so many animals that were spliced into each other that most of the animals upon the planet were not of the original creation. God was only bringing His original creation back to the ark. We stood there and watched the animals as they approached the ark.

Later, we saw Noah and his family loading animals on the boat. These animals were definitely peculiar. They were waiting basically in line to get on a boat. The numbering of them was just as described in

Scriptures. Of each animal there were two sets of two animals, male and female. The 'clean' animals had seven sets of two, male and female. We saw the door of the boat shut and sealed. The number of people going into the boat was eight. It was Noah's family.

Just then Jonathan and Samantha recognized Devorah-7C2 and Mr. Katool-0A3 walking toward us. Jonathan asked about her reasoning for being here. She said that it was because our lives are in danger. The flood is coming soon. Before the flood comes, the citizens of the neighboring town will swarm upon this place trying to escape the flood. She told us that we needed to hurry. So, we hurried to the archways and returned.

Moments after returning to the cube, we disconnected level-three time travel. We sat and talked with her and the cat for awhile. We asked her how she got here, and she said that they always have a 'key' to our cube and there are others that they created. It was time for her to leave, she had accomplished her mission. She told us that she would see us again. She knew that we would not be able to resist using the cube to look into the distant past, and into the distant future. However, we did not know what she meant. As she was about to vanish from our sight, she bid us farewell and then faded into the sky-blue light of the cube.

Curiosity grabbed us again. We wanted to see the Tower of Babel for ourselves and its destruction. Therefore, we pushed the lever away from the notch toward the operator gently. We did not want to get involved with the people there. We just wanted to observe the event, so we stayed in level-two time travel mode. We watched them trying to finish building the structure, it was huge. But it was not as impressive as the buildings before the flood.

We noticed a commotion occurring at the building site. It was Noah and his sons! They were trying to tell them not to build the tower. Noah tried to reason with them; telling them that God told them to disperse. Their response was that they did not hear Him and that the story of the flood was some kind of fairytale. After this, they were driven off the site by the workers under the direction of Nimrod.

Noah and his family were saddened by the hard-headedness of over 90 percent of their offspring. In fact, there was only family line that listened. That line led to Eber. It was at the birth of his son Peleg that God allowed the division of the Earth to unfold.

While these people were working hard day and night, Earth was getting closer to Jupiter. They were working up to the day that there was a severe electrical storm. During that very day, people became confused and could not understand each other. People would be hard at work until they reached a point of needing more material, help or information. They attempted to communicate with each other about their need for the project. This was of no avail. At first, they thought that their plight was some kind of joke being played upon them. Frustrated with their dilemma, they stopped working on the project. They were perplexed at the complexity of trying to accomplish a simple task. They began to express anger toward each other because they could not communicate.

Interestingly enough, there were groups of people that could understand each other, and these groups separated themselves from the rest of whom they could not understand. However, there was one group of people which did not have their language confused. Noah and the family line that remained with him did not have their language confused. They were the ones not working on the tower; their language became labeled as Hebrew. This was because this was the language that Eber spoke. The language was named after him. Eber was the great grandson of Noah. It was from the Hebrew root meaning to cross over. Ironically, this is the language that 'crossed over' from the flood.

Eventually, these groups were not content with living in the same vicinity as other groups speaking a different language. They decided to separate themselves further by journeying away from each other. Sure enough, within that year there was an earthquake that lasted for the entire day at the birth of Peleg. The entire landmass was divided as we had witnessed earlier.

We had a lot of information to input into our report. So, we returned to the cube through our respective archways. I was still intrigued by the idea that Noah was there during the time of the Tower of Babel. Secondly, I was astonished at the disrespect that was shown to Noah by his relatives.

Everyone but Joseph, wanted to go home. He wanted to go back further and talk to Adam. After debating the issue, curiosity got the best of us once again. I remembered observing Devorah-7C3 setting the time using the keyboard. I went to the consol and entered a number to represent -1,500 years using the keyboard. It was nerve-racking. First obstacle was that they operated in base sixty instead of our base ten. I calculated the number for conversion; the digits were 25 and 0. The second obstacle was that I had to be certain of the characters that I typed. They were all very foreign to me. What does the character digit 25 look like. One the side of the keyboard was a numbering pad with sixty keys arranged in a six by ten array. Which key would be the convention for zero? However, I managed to enter the right characters. We ended up back in the time just after the fall of mankind.

After arriving there, we entered through the archways in mode three. We saw the dome-like field and knew that we were still close to the Garden of Eden. We searched around the dome to find its entrance. There was no fence around the dome or any weapons of Node. We were a little distance from the entrance of the dome. We observed two figures facing the gate. We walked up behind them. Startled, they turned around.

We asked them their name. They seemed puzzled by the question. They said that they were Adam and Eve. They pointed out their two sons playing just outside the Gadedan Providence. They returned to look at its closed gate. They both looked somewhat sad while the children were playing, who seemed oblivious to their parents' sadness. We examined their surroundings. While the immediate landscape was beautiful, there were no major skyscraper cities to be seen on the skyline of the horizon. However, there were paved roads leading away from the gate. I was thinking, "How could there be paved roads?" My curiosity got the best of me, again. I asked Adam about the roads and where do they come from? He told me that the people of Node (Nod) built them about a thousand years ago, while he was still in the garden. He said that the people of Node were somewhat primitive in nature. However, they were teachable.

He questioned us about who we were. He told us that we looked like one that was transformed, but he had never seen us before today. He said that he knew everyone of this kind personally. The questions that floored me were "Transformed? Transformed from what? Everyone? That means they are not the only ones."

Joseph interrupted me as I had composed my question in my head and was ready to speak. He asked. "How long were you both in the garden?" Adam answered that it was about 7,000 years for him, and his wife was there for about 3,500 years. He said that if you wanted more details about his life in the garden, all we had to do is read the Star-Writings. We told him that we did not know how to read them. His reply was, "You really are not a natural citizen. We all can read the Star-Writings. Again, I ask you, where are you from?"

I told him that we were from the future. In fact, we were approximately 6,000 years into the future. His reply was that being 6,000 years into the future, we should be able to read these star-writings more efficiently. Then Jonathan expounded unto him, that there is some kind of decay that has occurred. We used machines to accomplish what we observe you doing. Within these writings we were instructed not to read the stars. The primary reason was perversions of the readings were implemented by our predecessors. We have writings that are called the Torah, Bible, or Word of God. He was comforted by that.

Joseph then asked him about the transformed ones. Adam said, "Before the fall. He would preach unto the people in Node. There would always be some that wanted to walk in the way of the Star-

Writings one they knew what they were. Actually, there were ten basic commandments." Joseph interrupts, "I know those." He smiled and said, "Good." He then continues to talk about those who he separated from Node.

He told us that they would take them into the garden to meet with God. We then would intercede on their behalf telling God that they wanted to be adopted into His family. Then God would place His hands on them through us. They would transform before their eyes. Then we realized that these people formed the nation of Ayd, which we became aware of on our previous journey.

Still puzzled, Joseph enquired about the transformation. He said that he and his wife both before the fall use to physically glow. It made a glowing white garment unto us. There were other physical modifications, but the most spectacular was the glowing skin. We brought thousands into the fold. After the fall, we all lost our glow and became affected by the external environment. Our physical bone structure was about the only aspect of ourselves that remained with us. We needed clothes, tools, and shelter. We also noted our mental faculties fading. That is probably the reason that you have the Star-Writings in books.. He also stated that he wasn't certain that the book writings could reflect all the three levels of Star-Writing.

Lastly, he spoke of his sorrow at being unable to reenter the garden. He and his wife would go to the entrance of the garden every seventh day. It was to remind themselves of the past glory days and contemplate their loss. He told us that he and his wife would at times break down and cry here. They were comforted by the Star-Writings. It tells them of a future hope of everything being made anew.

Joseph asked Adam, "Did it seem strange that the serpent was talking?" His reply was "No." Shocked by the response, Joseph asked "How is that not unusual?" Adam replied, "All animals talked with us at that time. We even talked to the beasts that were considered wild. I recall a certain white rabbit asking me for the correct time. I told him that it was noon. He was very upset; he said that he was late. I couldn't ascertain for what reason he was late. He just hopped away in such a rush. I am still puzzled by his response. The way those rabbits hop around everywhere so quickly, how can any rabbit ever be late? That was really crazy."

Samantha interjected, "Was he wearing a waistcoat?" Adam, perplexed by the question responded "What? No. Why should he be dressed in any clothing?" She apologized as she was snickering. Margo interjected, "Wait, wait, I got one. The rabbit calculated that the turtle was going to cross the finish line just before high noon. He was too late to finish the race!"

Adam looked at her in astonishment. He said, "A race? The rabbit is racing with a turtle? You all have some serious issues." Margo said that they are thinking of childhood stories.

Joseph then asked, "Can you talk with the animals now?" Adam said that only in a limited fashion, not like before. He said also that he missed that phenomenon as well, but not as much as his wife. However, we still enjoy being around them and taking care of them.

Then Joseph inquired about the feelings the people in Ayd had toward him. They were upset with me at first. God squelched their complaint. He told them that none of them would have done any better. I am comforted somewhat by it. However, I still wished that I would have kept His commandment. No matter how much I repent of the action, it will not reverse the effect. It is like breaking a glass bowl. It cannot be mended. Before the fall, I could have mended it, but not after.

Joseph wanted to ask more questions about the garden, but he held his peace. I told them that we really needed to get back home. Joseph reluctantly agreed. We bid Adam and Eve farewell and returned to the archways to the cube. We took all our recordings and catalogued them in chronological order and stored them in several thumb drives. We had a comfortable flight home. I slept most of the way home.

Information on the recording devices was taken to the universities to be analyzed. They wanted us to write our accounts as well. We wrote the information of our last journey down while it was fresh in our minds. All our information was deemed top secret up to the present day. We have little to no hope that it would ever be released. However, they could not undo the public knowledge of a time machine. They printed limited amounts of unessential material on the subject. It was far less than that which should have been printed. As for us, we had some more exploring to do because of our curiosity on other issues. We wanted to observe the beginning and the end of the universe. We were still puzzled by the expression that Devorah-7C2 referred to the end of 'this' universe. I was not sure if there was any such thing. Even though, she does not seem to be one to make idle statements.

Margo and I were making plans for our next journey into time. We said to each other that we should get input from our teammates. As we talked with other members of our team, we were trying to determine our next adventure should be. Ruth said that perhaps it would be good to start with the beginning. That made sense to me. George said that he would get a big bang out of it, pun intended. Samantha told him he may be surprised. There was a vote, and the beginning won. So, we made plans to return to Peru.

Chapter 9

Year Zero

Traveling to Peru made me reflect on the excitement that the world had when we announced that we were going on an expedition in time. Now, they are saying there they go again almost scoffing. Returning to the cube was almost like returning home. After reviewing the manual and the information that Devora-7C2 gave us, we were ready to consider our next designation. We decided earlier, we were going all the way back. At least as far as the time lever would let us. We pondered about what would be the marker for the beginning of time. Our logic was that any instant in time that we could imagine, there would be a time before that.

We remembered; we could not visit this location beyond level-one time traveling. After doing all the preparation, I pushed the time lever all the away from me. Again, we observed swirling multicolored misty lights and all the sounds. As the mist cleared away, we found ourselves in the sky-blue cube. Our first thought was that it did not work. Within ten seconds, Devorah-7C2 and Mr. Katool-0A3 appeared in the cube. What were they doing being here in the cube with us?

Both Devorah-7C2 and Mr. Katool-0A3 were glad to see us. They said their greetings in English. She told us that she knew that we could not resist going all the way back, because she saw it in all her journeys through time. They purposely came at this time to help us understand the phenomenon that we would be seeing. George asked her about the presence of the cat android. Her reply was that 0A3 (this is what she called Mr. Katool-0A3) was very intuitive. It would provide her with information concerning our ability to understand her message.

Questions kept popping into our minds. Perhaps one of the most prevalent questions was about their existence in the cube. She told us that she dialed the date in which we would press the lever totally toward hour zero. In this, they were truly here in the cube with us. Then the cat jumped into the lap of Ruth and started purring. Ruth then testified that truly there was a cat in her lap. This was not just a hologram.

Another nagging question was about our time jump. Did it truly occur or was there some malfunction. She assured us that the jump truly occurred. I asked, "Then why was the cube showing only this sky-blue color?" Her initial reply was asking if we believed in God. George's reply was, "Are we supposed to believe that the color of God is sky-blue?"

She smiled and replied, "No, silly. There are no photons to give us any color. The color you see is a representation. Look at the space between us. It is clear. Now, imagine having nothing to impede your vision from looking farther. You would see clear to infinity. What color would your eyes tell you that you are seeing? It would not be black because it is not clear. White would mean there was light. The color the mind might jump to is gray. Think of living color. Take a black and white picture of blue. You would get this particular color of gray. Why do you think the sky is blue?"

Cynthia replied, "Because of the molecules in the air."

Her response was "And why is that? Sure, you can talk about the light refractive properties of molecules using detail upon detail until you are blue in the face. No pun intended. All the while, you would be failing to see that it was by design."

George then replied, "Okay, so you have it clear out to infinity. It still does not mean that there is a God." Samantha told George to calm down and said that if he refuses to believe that there is a God, fine. Despite your angst about this issue, let us listen and understand.

This time Mr. Katool-0A3 responded. "We have developed sensors that are telepathic in nature. When we sent our sensors out into this void-like region, we sensed an intelligence like nothing else that we encountered in this universe. It was not in just one location, but it was everywhere."

Devorah-7C2 spoke "Obviously, some of you have issues over the existence of God. We do not need to debate the issue. We know that telepathic responses are alien to you. We should have known that this would be a touchy subject. Were you not coming here to experience hour zero? We haven't even started to show you the beginning of our universe. It would have been easier if you believed in God. The concepts won't have as much meaning, but we can continue."

I said, "Please do."

She then said, "What you are looking at is a time an instant before the existence of this universe. Perhaps, the best way to explain it is to imagine a plane of pixels on a computer screen. An empty universe would be represented as turning on the screen with no software. All the pixels would be displaying their version of black; there are no images and no variation of color. This is an empty universe. Turn the screen off, and you have time before the universe exists. This is the purpose of the blue that you observe. It is a time before light or darkness of this universe."

Mr. Katool-0A3 spoke up and said: "7C2, perhaps you should skip the creation of energy and go into the formulation of matter. Talking about its relationship between God and energy would be disturbing to some of them."

She looked disappointed; she said "I had a whole discourse prepared on the topic. I will say this; the first energy created was inertia. Then the attracting energy was created in which we get gravity, kinetic energy and finally repelling energy. We call it the repelling force heat or microstrong; your scientists call it the weak force. I suppose it is a matter of perspective. At any rate, it is responsible for keeping an electron from crashing into a proton. Lastly, the creation of magnetic energy is the interaction between the two types of energy. This means both positive and negative charges were created simultaneously."

Turning to me, she said that she needed to control the time lever. The purpose was not only to skip over the creation of energy, but to move it forward slowly as only a machine could. I was eager to observe zero hour. I got out of the chair and gave the consol over to her. She materialized a recliner for me to sit in by moving it from their time into the cube. She then had us lay down in our recliners to look up to the ceiling. As we did, an image gradually appeared above us. After looking at the image, she said, "I got a little ahead of myself talking of magnetic energy. Let's go back to a time before its creation.

Initially, the image we saw was a translucent cube. Within the cube the three-dimensional lines appeared they intersected each other in the center of the cube perpendicular to each other. Then we noticed that the space between these lines widening forming six funnels that merged to the six faces of the cube, one funnel per face. Next, we saw lines going upon the surface of the funnel from the center of the cube fanning out to the edge of each cubical face. Looking straight at any particular face, it appeared as many lines intersecting at the facial center, excusing the 3D effect. Then we noticed that the lines from one funnel were joined to the lines with the adjacent funnel at each cubical edge. Each funnel was connected with their respective adjacent funnels. Next, we noted that the joined lines met each other with no sudden bend. Lastly, we saw that each line was a string of dots moving in two directions within the line.

Devorah-7C2 described the image as geysers erupting from the cubical core per dimensional face. The energy flows from one face into the four adjacent funnels back to the core for the apparent eruption within the opposite funnel. This is a continuous motion for all six faces of the cube. The cube that we observed was tremendously enlarged. This was the image of the smallest particle in the universe. She called it a xyzenthium (pronounced Size.enth.i.um) crystal which was in other words a sub-neutron particle. Another item she said about the xyzenthium cube is that the crystal's dimensions can be compressed. However, if was allowed, it would expand until it engulfed the entire universe.

She then said, "Now we are going to see the transformation of the crystal into a magnetic crystal." Off to the side a rectangular frame expanded into existence. Within this frame we saw a line with dots traveling two directions in a single line. The dots of both directions of motion were the same color, purple. Then we noticed that one set of dots turned blue and the other moving the opposite direction turned red. Then we saw the change within the crystal. Then we observed that another transformation occurred. One funnel had primarily red dots flowing in and out, with the opposite funnel having primarily blue dots flowing in and out. Another set of opposing funnels having primarily red dots flowing in with blue dots flowing out. Lastly, the other set had blue dots flowing in and red dots flowing out.

George interrupted, "What caused the dots to change color?"

Devorah-7C2 said firmly, "Whether or not, you believe God is responsible for this transformation is irrelevant. The writings state that He divided the light from the darkness. This is the scientific ramification of His action at the most basic level, among other ramifications. This is written. Keeping out all the technical details, we will view it as a multitude of two-dot objects flowing through one line. Each two-dot object has a blue dot and a red dot. Going left, the red dot is on top and blue on the bottom. Going right, the colors are flipped. When these objects come into contact each dot transfers its color. Red becomes blue and the red one blue. In "dividing light from darkness," only one side transfers. For convenience, let's say the bottom dots do not transfer. Kind of a 'hiccup' in the process the blue dot remains blue. The red dot remains red. However, the top dots continue their process, i.e., the blue becomes red, and the red becomes blue. This happens for one interval. The result is that there are now two blue dots moving in one direction, and two red dots moving in the opposite direction."

Visualization of the cubical crystal changed into a solid for purposes of analyzing the crystal using a different set of colors. Instead of all the faces of the cube being a blue color, this time two opposite faces were green, and another two opposite faces were red. The remaining two faces were yellow. However, the yellow faces were of two different shades, one light and the other dark. The cube was rotating so that we could verify the arrangement. She stopped the image.

She said to us that we were witnessing the transformation of the crystal into a magnetic crystal. The red represents the negative magnetic charge, the green represents the positive charge, and the yellow faces are neutrally charged. The light yellow is the microstrong force and the dark yellow is the microweak force. These crystals form layers. If the layer shows red, then it is a negatively charged layer. There was only one layer type that is not purely one color; it is primarily a red and green checkered neutral layer. It is one of three neutral layers. The others being light yellow layer and a dark yellow layer. The charge of a given layer depends upon the crystal alignment.

Continuing with the demonstration, we saw layers forming stacked upon each other in the same pattern for the six different facial directions. In essence the entire universe was divided into cubes. We were told that each neutron cube had approximately ten trillion cubes. We will not go into the details on how the layers join only that one single layer alignment forms per cubical surface. The image then appears as a universe of cubical neutrons that are squarely in contact with each other. The outer three layers of each neutron have dark yellow faces facing out. The neutral layers internally cause the neutron to shrink as these have positive and negative faces pulling the layer together. The cube shrinks into a spherical- like neutron. Left alone, the result would be a universe would be filled with uniformly spaced neutrons, then afterward this would transform into a universe of hydrogen gas.

Preventing that to occur, a single neutron was moved out of place breaking the isometric hold upon each neutron. This moved neutron becomes closer to other neutrons in the direction of the movement. Behind the movement, the space between it and the neutrons behind it becomes greater. The greater the distance creates a weaker hold. The neutrons behind the neutrons left behind, become closer to each other than to the neutron that was moved. At this point, gravity takes over. The result is that the central neutrons move away from each other as they are pulled away further from the center via gravity. The speed increases as it pulls away from the center. Another interesting effect is that the neutrons clump together. Further away from the center they form larger clumps. It is like a pebble thrown into the water; the waves get wider as they leave the center.

Formulation of a thin shelled sphere forms expanding from the center. After some point, the mass of the spherical shell becomes greater than the pull of the external universe which was causing the spherical ring to grow in both diameter and in mass as it collects neutron clumps. The mass pulls the external neutron clumps into itself. The Hebrew term firmament becomes meaningful, as it means to hammer thin.

Pulling neutrons from outside the growing sphere had the inverse effect. The first clumps of neutrons were big and dwindled in size as the sphere continues to grow. Eventually, the heaviest material is found in the center of the shell. As the neutrons were being pulled into the shell, the clumps became smaller and smaller. Toward the end, only helium and hydrogen atoms were forming outside the shell. Finally, there was a great quantity of hydrogen gas forming external to the shell. This occurs because the neutrons formed into protons before they could be pulled into the shell. This is why there are large quantities of hydrogen in the universe.

Another interesting feature is that radioactive material forms at the exact moment that the shell mass was no longer being pulled by the multitude of external neutrons. A thin layer of neutrons formed joins the already formed clump of neutrons. The clump had already determined a pattern of neutrons and protons, and this layer 'did not comply.' At this point we zoom out into the macro universe. We observed not just one growing spherical shell mass, but we observe a multitude of these occurrences. Each expanding spherical shell held a multitude of galaxies. As the sphere continues its expansion, without adding more mass to itself the shell thins and breaks into separate galaxies. Within each galaxy there was further breakup of the mass into stars and planets.

Besides this phenomenon, there are two more to explore. First to discuss is the anti-shell phenomenon. Recall the growing spheres of mass. If we were to line up spheres beside each other, not all the available space is absorbed by the spheres. There are spaces between spheres. Neutrons within this space will pull together. These will form neutron stars. The matter is so dense that light is unable to escape. The opposite of this is when matter in the galactic shell has optimum collection ability, quasars form. Light bends around the quasar as it is racing through space near the velocity of light. Behind the quasar, the light crashes into itself forming a tail a little distance away from the quasar.

Devorah-7C2 then says "This concludes our tour of the micro-formation of hour zero. Are there any questions?"

My curiosity got the best of me, and I just had to ask, "How do neutrons turn into protons. Truly, it cannot be by some magical accomplishment."

The cat gave a Cheshire smile and said, "Ah, curiosity killed the cat. You will definitely be getting some science."

She said, "You asked for it… Recall that the three outermost layers of the neutron were composed of an alignment in which the dark yellow sides of the xyzenthium crystal were facing out. Secondly, this layer contracts the neutron form from a cube into a sphere. The bulging mass is from the pressure inside the neutron. These three layers are not the only neutral layers. There are sequences of layers that exists underneath these three incorporated alignments.

However, the bulging pressure is not the force that removes the outer three layers of the neutron. The backside of the dark yellow layer is light yellow. This represents the microstrong force. The microstrong force is a repelling force. Being in micro-space, it is extremely strong.

It is constantly pushing out. The crystals are ejected from the surface forming gamma rays. Because of their mass in comparison to light waves, they are harmful. After these three surfaces evaporate off the surface, the negative charged layer is exposed.

Under the negative layer (red) that will eventually be the surface of an electron, is another dark yellow layer. Under this layer, is layer is a green layer, representing a positive charged alignment. The positive charged layer emits microstrong particles as does the layer above it emit the same energy against it. We call this the hyper-push. Since the three layers that were holding the push back have evaporated. The repelling force wins and expels the two layers forming the electron. As it is expelling the electron the secondary layer rips a small patch from its layer forming neutrinos. The neutrino evaporates and forms more gamma radiation. The electron becomes a large shell collecting microstrong energy in the form of heat energy from the nucleus. The remaining surface on the original neutron now becomes a positive charged proton."

She said additionally, "I will expound a little on the nature of an electron. The electron has an isobaric spin to it. As it is being pulled into the proton, the electron is gathering heat of the microstrong energy radiating from the nucleus into its large internal chamber. As it falls toward the proton, microstrong energy pushes back upon the electron. As it is being ejected away, the electron is pushed beyond the limit of the prevailing influence of the microstrong energy. The electron cools. Its outer shell contracts, and the door, located where the layer tore away over the mass of the neutron slides apart over the hole generated by the neutrino. A photon is ejected from the electron. The door closes, and the process starts again."

She asked again, "Anymore questions?"

We kept our mouths shut. She said, "Good. Let's continue into the experience."

Zooming out and focusing upon one of the shells of galaxies, we noted that some of the galaxies from one sphere passed through another galaxy from another sphere without much interference. Occasionally, we saw stars crashing into each other. The way they crashed was somewhat peculiar. We observed three manifestations within the crash. A central circular plane expanded from the center. Two butterfly wing-like structures formed one on each side of the central plane. These also grew. She told us that the central plane formed as the velocities of the two stars canceled out leaving the horizontal part of their vectors involved in the motion. The two 'butterfly wings' were caused by the kinetic energy of the two stars passing through the collision.

Focusing on one star-storm, incidentally, it was ours. We observed the formation of our solar system. It looked like a hurricane. The main difference was that the center of the storm did not have a hollow eye but was a little thicker. This storm had three arms spinning out from it. Each leg was formed by its attachment to another star. These legs broke away as our solar storm swirled. There was a solar disc that reached out as far as the average distance the asteroid belt is from the present-day sun. This disc contracts toward being a sphere. As the solar material contracts, three noticeable masses of spinning storms emerge near the sun.

The biggest of the plasmatic storms was the one forming the earth. It was second from the solar disc. The central disc to these storms was contracting as well. There was no plasmatic storm formulating the moon next to it. Devorah-7C2 focused in on the plasmatic storm forming earth. We observed the disc as it shrunk into a sphere. The sphere was molten. The outer surface of the sphere started forming a thin crust. Looking over the top of the rotational axis, we saw a spiral forming on the crust. It was somewhat lighter in color. She said this spiral is called Havilah in her language. We were also told that the atmosphere surrounding the sphere was nearly 250 times that of the present day.

The side of the storm that was facing outward of the expanding shell of galaxies had slightly more material than the rest of the sphere. There was about 14,000 feet of material that sunk into the spherical mass of the planet. In the center of this layer, its elevation was about 500 feet. At the edge, it was nearly zero feet above 14,000 feet. This material was slightly lighter than the rest of the spherical surface. This region cooled first.

We zoomed in on the lighter surface. Since we were not there in time travel level-two or three, we were not singed by the hot atmosphere above the boiling point of water. But this was about to change. We looked upon the surface and saw moister condensation forming on the rocks as if the rocks were sweating.

Eventually, water collected and formed streams down the edge. As the streams formed, some of the surface material was washed down with the water causing the streams to cut into the soil. Flowing off the lighter mass into a heavier and hotter basin, steam would rise violently cooling the region in which it came into contact. Eventually, puddles formed. Some time later, the water puddles joined together and covered the entire surface. Meanwhile, the water continued to collect upon the surface of the water. Then we saw a single ocean covering the whole earth as we zoomed back out into space. Mr. Katool- 0A3 spoke up and told us the atmospheric pressure was now only ten times of our present time atmospheric pressure.

There was another phenomenon that altered the surface. We went back down to the surface under the water. The earth moved back away from the solar disc. The earth was shaken by a large quake. The surface tension was becoming greater. This shelf cracked at the edge and the landmass arose out of the water. We came back out of the water and back into space. We could see the landmass as a disc on the bottom of the planet tilted slightly to one side. This is the same image seen that Samantha observed when they left for Mars!

George asked, "What caused the Earth to move away from the sun and the earthquake?"

She answered him, "Don't ask questions that you do not want to know the answer to. However, to answer your question, this would involve God."

"So, this is year zero on the earth!" exclaimed Cynthia. Then Devorah-7C2 interjected, "You mean that you do not wish to see the formation of plants and animals?"

Cynthia replied, "I didn't mean that. Yes, I would like to see how plants and animals were created."

Devorah-7C2 response was, "This kind of information also requires the acknowledgement of God. Are you ready for such a shift of your psychological composition?" Cynthia said that she was willing to listen without interjecting opposition. Then George asked for a vote. He was out voted. Then he resigned himself to the popular vote.

Again, we went back down to the surface of the empty and now dry ground. We noticed that a thin membrane forming in one of the archways. She sent out a tiny machine through the membrane out to the landscape. We watched as the machine phased through the membrane. The machine scooped up a sample of the soil and brought it back to the cube to analyze its content. The soil seemed to be like granite. The difference was that the cubical checkered pattern was between organic and inorganic matter. The primary elements of organic matter were carbon, oxygen, and hydrogen with trace amounts of different elements.

Watching as she placed the sample into a small cubical crystal box and placing it into the lower bottom on the left side of the screen into an indentation, she told us that we needed to get back into the recliners and look up at the sky-blue ceiling. We did. We saw movement within the organic region of the soil. We saw patterns of movement that tightened into an oval seed. She said, the movement that you saw was generated by God.

The tiny machine took the seed and planted it. After it returned through the membrane, the membrane disappeared. She said that all life on earth formed somewhat in a similar manner. Some formed under water becoming sea creatures.

Viewing the landscape from the cube again, we saw to our surprise that there were already plants outside. We thought it was nighttime, but it lasted far beyond 24 hours. She pointed to the sky behind us. There we saw it, a large flattened glowing red ellipsoid. We asked her, "What object is that?" She told us that it was the sun.

Turning back to her in disbelief George spoke up, "The Sun?" She smiled and told us to look at the landscape and tell her what we saw. We replied that we saw a black sky, red ground, and plants with black leaves. She said in return that the sun is like a darkroom light for photography that keeps the room dark. The leaves are not black but green. If you shine a red light on a green pigment, all that is seen is black. This is because green absorbs the red light. The reason for the sun to be red is that it is still in a pure plasmatic state.

Returning out into space, we looked and noticed that there was no moon. She said that it was coming, and that is the reason for bringing us back out into space. Sure enough, there was a comet coming toward the sun. She told us that she would speed up time for us so that we could observe the process.

This comet was spinning upon its axis as it was moving toward the sun. The atmosphere was frozen onto its surface but was misting and becoming an atmosphere again. As the planet moved closer to the sun than the earth, we saw that the atmosphere was vaporizing and being blown off by the solar wind. Then we saw the surface of the planet boiling, eventually all the surface was boiling. The vapors again were blown off by the friction of moving toward the sun. It passed the orbit of Mercury by a fraction. We saw where the top layer had been vaporized and blown back away into space. We also observed that its rotation slowed to a stop. It also moved in slight counter rotation back and forth before it stopped. Finally, the planet was moving away from the sun and toward earth; and it was captured by the earth.

Cynthia said that she had one question. "What caused the moons rotation to slow down?" We agreed that it was a good question. The response from Devorah-7C2 was that the core of the moon was like thick water partially filling a ball inside. Friction from the gravity and the solar wind pushed this liquid to one side. Gravity shifted affected by this movement and holds the 'water' to always face the front towards the sun. The liquefied core is much cooler and denser than a plasmatic core and takes up less room within the lunar shell. The mass resists moving with the rotation. The momentum of the shell kept trying to rotate. Toward the end of the scenario, there was a rocking back and forth of the rotation. After rotating forward a little, and then it was pulled back to the optimum gravitational pull which is the side facing the sun. The friction of the thick liquid against the outer shell causes the process to stop into stillness.

Core temperature of the moon drops; this caused the liquid facing the interior floor surface to solidify holding the moon's gravity in a stationary position. The quote unquote empty space under the surface is not empty. There are gases filling the 'would be void'; they are primarily krypton, xenon, argon with traces of other gases. This was the initial reason that the human population had us machines mining in the cavern. We do not need oxygen to breathe, nor do we tire of labor, at least in the way that the humans did. Our tiring was measured in the degradation of the molecular formation required to perform the given task. Later the reason became that of being cost effective. Especially when the cost of creating an android went down, they became intoxicated with making more money and with less effort.

Acknowledging the awe of the spectacle, George spoke up and said that the chances of the moon being captured that way were astronomical. She said "You are right. In fact, it is nearly impossible. Once again, it was an act of God."

She let us watch the sun turn from a red flattened ellipsoid that had a central ridge into a near spherical form. As it did so, it turned white. She told us that the plasma of the sun had to cool down to emit the photons of different wavelengths causing by additive coloring giving the appearance of white. Before that occurrence, only red could be seen from the solar plasma. There is a seemly contradiction saying that we like, just because it is so contradictory. It is like a pun for us. The sun had to cool to ignite. Crazy right?

She continued, "After the sun ignited, animal forms were created." We saw upon the surface partially buried eggs and buried eggs hatching. Birds came out of the shell and flew. Underwater, we saw the same phenomenon. Except fish were coming out of their shells and swimming away. She said, "This answers your riddle, 'Which came first, the chicken or the egg?' The answer is the egg, but it was not laid by a chicken." Then she snickered.

George then asked, "What caused the differentiation of bird and fish?"

She replied, "I told you. Do not ask questions that you do not want to know the answer to. However, I will answer. It was God that determined which seed formed a plant, a bird or a fish. Moreover, the different species of each are determined by Him. To God, each seed or organic granule within the earth contains all the elements needed to formulate organic forms. These forms are houses for life, not life itself. Life is another issue. However, if you are referring to the actual organic chemical processes that occurred. That would take even more time on topics that are biological in nature. That knowledge is beyond me. In that regard, I am more concerned with the mechanical makeup of androids, such as myself. I have knowledge of the bonding of atoms into many molecular compositions. However, the biological configurations and their relationship to life, this I have no knowledge. It is beyond mere chemical configurations."

After a brief pause, she said we can continue to watch the progression of creation. Next on my list is the creation of land animals. Then she asked, "Do you wish to continue?"

We said to her that we were exhausted and would like to return home. She agreed that it was much to absorb. We got back into our recliners and activated the machine's travel mechanism. Then she brought us back to our time. She told us that she was going back to her time to the time where the notch was placed. We watched as she and her cat both disappeared. We went back home ourselves pondering both that which we saw and that which we heard.

Chapter 10

The End

According to my logic, there was one more 'must take' journey. That was to go all the way into the future. I talked to the others about doing this journey. Most of them agreed that the journey would satisfy their nagging desire to know. Some of them were a little apprehensive about knowing the future. Primarily, they had a bad feeling that they would not like the facts. Among those was Samantha. Her feelings had the worst ring to it. She pointed out the negative elements of life seem to prevail. I pointed out that the last major war ended the rise of another evil takeover in 2025. Even though the war was horrific, and many died. The threat was removed. She retorted that our society was heading in a downward spiral again. I had to acknowledge that she was right. Lastly, I brought up Noah, which was the worst destruction ever. I noted that good would remain. It reminded them that evil truly was not in control, but God. With that they reluctantly reconsidered their positions and agreed to go. Even George agreed, who did not like my argument. Even so, they wanted to take a break from their time traveling. So, we went home.

Traveling back to Peru again was pleasant. We had a straight flight from Los Angeles to Lima. Gomez met us at the airport and took us directly to the cube. We remembered not to time travel at levels two or three. When I started to move the time lever, Devorah-7C2 and Katool-0A3 appeared in the cube again. I released the time lever and let it return to its original position. We were wondering why

134

they reappeared. The cat loved Samantha and hopped back into her lap. Devorah-7C2 said that they knew that we were planning to push the lever to its future limit. This was because once again, they saw us do it long ago.

Giving the standard warning about using level-two and three, she paused for a moment. She looked at us and asked, "Do you really want to push the lever all the way to its limit?" She issued another warning saying that the future of this universe is not about the advancement of the human race. It was absolutely terrifying for the machines. It means their end. I told you before, that some of you will be able to leap beyond this universe while others will be stuck in a place where they would not want to go. Our reply was that we were not certain that we would like the results, but we still would like to know.

She replied that our response was a shaky response. She asked for the control of the time lever and its components. She brought in another recliner device for me. I gave her control of the console and hooked myself into the recliner. The swirling colors and noises filled the cube. This time when the colored mist faded, there was no image appearing to view. All there was to observe was a painfully bright white light. She saw that we were in misery and released the lever and unplugged our connection to the machine. The room gradually returned to its sky-blue color. She said that our observation was that of the end of this universe. That image is not just on earth but everywhere in the entire universe. She said that if we could go further from this point, we would see this universe fade, and another takes its place. But we cannot go further because we would no longer be in this universe. The cube cannot take anyone there. It is the end of its function.

George asked, "How do you know all this?" She replied that because it is. We have tried. Look at the three obelisks. The energy glow of the crystals is at the top of the top panel. There are no more crystals that can be activated. Then paused, and then said that if you referring to the idea that there is a following universe. It has been written in the stars for ages. Even in your Scriptures, it speaks of this.

Everyone looked disappointed that the only image they saw was the bright light. She perceived their response as to be saying they wanted to see more. She then told them that they needed to see the absolute end of this universe before seeing the events that happened just before this universe reached its end and the hope of another universe following it. She asked us to return our recliners, and we did. She then nudged the time lever to a time just before the end.

Again, the swirling colors returned and faded. This time an image of a city appeared. The architecture was like the one we saw before the flood. The buildings looked well maintained. The machinery in the city was different. Electricity and magnetism along with mechanical mechanisms seem to be the primary source for energy, not crystal operated machinery. Although they were using crystals, they were used to store data and for containing operating programs. We went into the major cities and saw that there was no graffiti on the buildings. The streets were well maintained as well. Their vehicles were also well maintained and colorful. The people that we saw were well dressed, courteous and well behaved.

Our next objective was to investigate their monetary system. We saw a bank. We entered in. Being at level-one time traveling, no one saw or heard us. Up front at the cashier station, we saw people handing something that looked like a key to the teller. At closer examination, we saw a tiny crystal at the end of the key-like object. She told us that the crystal contained financial data among other information. This individual was making a payment on a loan in person. Security guards, at least they appeared to be, were assisting people with their requests outside the financial function of the bank.

Next stop was the universities. They had some beautiful structures for buildings. We went into the main office building to examine their curriculum. Their genetic classes were not inclusive of genetic splicing or alterations. Their primary study was the nature of genetic material. For example: what code makes a monkey, or a giraffe. On the human side, they were examining the different codes that make human nature different between human beings. There were also studies concerning the compositions of planets and moons. Space travel was another topic. Again, the people were nice in appearance, and nice to each other.

Joseph asked her about their religious practices. So, she took us to another building, it was huge and well designed. We went inside, and we saw a bulletin board. They worshipped on Saturday instead of Sunday. Joseph thought they were in a Jewish synagogue. Then she took them to several other religious buildings, they were all worshipping on Saturday. Then he saw the song list. The word 'Yeshua' was within one of the song titles. Yeshua is the Hebrew name of Jesus. He knew of the sect of Christianity that this information was describing- Messianic Judaism. This sect did not have many large congregations in his time era. Here, they are everywhere! We went into one of their Saturday services. Everyone there was into the service.

Within their judicial system, there were many elements that seemed severe. It was a very strict system. The penalties for minor crimes required seemingly heavy restitution. Violations that don't exist in our culture are heavily weighted. For example, divorce is a crime. The person found to be at fault had to spend time in jail. Dishonest dealings with other people also required jail time. However, there was a scale in which the severity of the crime was measured. From this scale, judgment was meted to the individual. Corporate crimes resulted in the annihilation of the corporation or that the corporation was handed over to another who was not part of the corporation. The reason for survival is because jobs are involved. We saw no provision of corruption. In fact, a judge found to be taking a bribe was also sentenced to spend time in jail and had to make payments of restitution.

Politics was also peculiar. For the most part there weren't any. There were no two-party systems anywhere. There were no national dictatorships. However, there was an existence of a central government. The system was called a theocracy. After a little research, we found that the ruler turned out to be Yeshua himself. He ruled from Jerusalem. He appointed leaders over the individual nations. These leaders enforced the dictates of the theocracy. These leaders had people under them controlling subsections of the country. The people seem to be genuinely happy. There were skirmishes that occurred from time to time, but they were quickly resolved.

The physical well-being of these people was also amazing. Virtually, no one had died for over 900 years. This was truly unbelievable. Health issues were nonexistent. The only problem was an occasional accident. Usually, it was because someone became overtaken by anger and did something stupid. Even so, this was stupendous. Longevity of life was somewhat reminiscent of the 'notch' era.

I was totally impressed by the culture that I saw. It was not just me, but nearly all our crew. We wondered whether this culture continued until the end of the universe. I ventured out to say, "This makes a great ending to the human race." Then Devorah- 7C2 spoke up. She said, "This is not the end. True, we are looking at the last days of the universe. However, this is not the end. There is more to come. I will show you." She then moved the time lever almost to the limit toward her.

We went back to the same location, Lincoln, Nebraska. It was Saturday, we went to the synagogue. While we were there, we noticed that it was not as full as it once was. We then heard some of practitioners talking in the back of the sanctuary. They were grumbling about the service. One was saying that the service was too long. Another one said that they did not like the message. I was perplexed by their responses. Last time that I was here, everyone was attentive to the service. I personally was disappointed.

Samantha said the universities would be a good place to get a feel of the psychological composition of the society. The rest of us agreed. So, we went to the university. While we were there, there was a protest rally. Stunned at the sight, from the data that we had earlier, there was no such thing for centuries. What brought this behavior into existence? We saw one of the fliers lying on the ground. We could not pick it up as we were in level-one time travel. However, we saw the large writing saying, Free your mind! Samantha said, "That tells all. These people were in rebellion." She said that because this was a pattern used in the 1960's to tear down the moral values of that time. There were pointless movements that wanted to tear down the existing system without any thought of what was going to replace it.

Devorah-7C2 told us that she was going to nudge the time lever a little more toward the end. We agreed, we saw enough here. The swirling colors came momentarily, and then it faded away again quickly. Going back to the synagogue on Saturday, we saw very few people showing up. The atmosphere changed from being joyful to that of being very somber. The service became more about praying for the community for its deeds was despicable. We were able to investigate other synagogues and found the same scenario. Again, this was very disturbing.

Wondering how badly this was reflected in the universities, we went back to Lincoln's major university. Again, there were protest rallies. This time we observed teachers involved promoting their causes against the theocracy. Looking at another flier, we saw the words 'Stand against the regime.' We heard people talking about weapon building for the cause.

Others were talking about the need for a revolution. Yet others talking crazy talk that did not have any logic to it at all. They were saying that the rules of the government are unjust. It was their lives; they should be able to do with it whatever feels right to them. They also wanted independence from the central government. They liken the government to 'the Evil Empire."

Within the city itself, we noted graffiti on the walls of buildings; they were primarily tags by gangs. Litter on the streets became prevalent. The people were no longer being courteous toward one another. This was a definite downturn in society. This behavior reflects somewhat the behavior of our own society. Devorah-7C2 said that it is not yet the end. She needed to nudge the lever two more times.

After the transition, we found ourselves back in the city of Lincoln. We entered the synagogue again. This would be the next to the last time that we visited this place. There were even less people than there were before. The service was short. We hated to think of the condition which this place would be next time. At the end of the service, a political message was read from the podium sent from Yeshua himself. He said that the end is near. There were planes waiting for those who desired to remain aligned with Him. They were to return to Jerusalem with the dignitaries that He sent to rule over them.

Back at the university, we looked at the curriculum. Even this was affected by the prevalent attitude of society. They had courses in what they called "Newthink." They had their 'social warriors.' They banned Scriptures from their libraries. Then we walked through the parkway to the universities. We could see graffiti on the sidewalks on the buildings, and places where there were broken glass windows from rocks being thrown. It truly was despicable. She asked us, "Seen enough?" All of us nodded yes.

Within the cube, we held a meeting concerning whether to continue going forward into time. Our last experience was heart wrenching to us. Some of us did not want to continue. They said that they could see that their path was leading to war. The rest of us wanted to continue. While there may be war, we wanted to see the outcome. The cat said that we should not be apprehensive. Our lives are not involved in whatever violence takes place. This is the far future. Whatever you see and write about will be long forgotten by these people. Just observe and report it to your people, it may do them good. The logic sounded good to us. We decided to continue. Katool-0A3 looked toward Devorah-7C2 and nodded his head, indicating for her to continue.

Afterward Devorah-7C2 moved toward the lever, we braced ourselves. She nudged it again. The swirling colors looked different; there were more red hues in them. The sounds were more disturbing. It sounded like yelling, screaming, and crying. I guess even the cube was setting a melodramatic mood for the event. The colored misted cleared, and we were back in Lincoln. The place looked even worse than before. It was beyond that I have ever seen before. The streets were dilapidated. The whole place looked dirty with trash being seen no matter where we looked. As far as the graffiti was concerned, there were several layers of it. People in the streets were dressed poorly. We witnessed an attempted robbery in the downtown region of the city.

Saturday came around, so we decided to go to the synagogue. There were broken windows and graffiti on the outer walls. We went inside and saw more graffiti, and not just one layer. Moreover, there was no one in the synagogue. We went up to the podium. We found a drawer under the podium's desk. There was a message written on a piece of paper. Using a mirror, we read it. It stated, 'If you are reading this, you need to leave and go to Jerusalem.' I thought that this might be a good idea. But Samantha wanted to check the university. So, we went back.

Wondering what we would find, we entered the building. There were not many people there either. There was, however, a counter enlisting people for the war. There were people standing in line. They said to each other the time for battle is at hand. A sign was overhead of the counter. It read, 'Join Now and Win your Freedom." Samantha asked, "People actually believe this?" This ended our tour in Lincoln. We decided that we needed to go to Jerusalem. She moved our location lever to view Jerusalem. We wanted upgrade or travel mode to level-two. The androids were not okay with this, as we were soon going to observe the evaporation of the universe.

Viewing the city of Jerusalem, we saw many people. The number of people was not as many as we thought there would be. True, there was a multitude, but this is all the people from the entire planet. It would have been overcrowded with people. We saw off to the distance hoards of people gathering outside the city. They all had weapons, even tank-like vehicles, hovercrafts with weapons exposed. Eventually, they got themselves into position for battle. They were waiting for orders to attack. As the orders to fire came, there shot vertical rays of light at the edge of Jerusalem. Whether it shot upward or downward we did not know which.

Suddenly, Devorah-7C2 moved us out far into space above Jerusalem. We saw that these vertical light rays formed a ring around

Jerusalem. This ring slowly expanded away from Jerusalem. Nothing passed through this ring of light. I saw the crowd of people shoot missiles toward Jerusalem. None of them passed through this ring. As the ring expanded, the region that it moved over left nothing but burning ashes. It seemed not to matter whether it was land or sea. Destruction occurred at sea as well, ships burned and sank. The ring kept on expanding until it reached the opposite side of the planet. The planet's landmasses looked blackish red except at Jerusalem. Steam was rising from the seas.

Afterward, the ring expanded again from the opposite side of the planet. Instead of being just a ring, the formulation was an expanding disc. She brought us down to Jerusalem. We saw the people there turn snow white and then they faded until they vanished from the surface of the earth. Meanwhile, the disc continues to expand. It even engulfed Jerusalem.

Shocked, we asked Devorah-7C2, "What happened to the people in Jerusalem?" Her reply was that they were translated into a parallel universe. As we looked at our surroundings, we saw the ban of light close in toward the center. Now, there was nothing left on earth. Then we noticed that white light was radiating from the earth. This light got brighter and brighter until we could not tolerate looking at it. This is the same image we initially saw when we pushed the time lever to its limit.

Returning to our existence within the cube, she said to us "Now you know the fate of the earth." Devorah-7C2 also warned us not to go into our near future. She said that it is very unpleasant. I do not know if she said that to spark our interest or if it was a genuine warning. But as for me, I had to know. Maybe we could avoid this unpleasantness because it hasn't happened yet. On the other hand, it sounded like she knew the answer to that scenario. Perhaps, the future is as unchangeable as the past. I was not going to ask her, because I did not want to know the answer. However, I could feel another journey coming up in by bones.

She looked at Katool-0A3 and said, "Come on 0A3, let us go home." She looked at us and said, "Before I leave; I want to take you to another location of time. She moved the time lever away from her about a sixth of the distance that the lever could travel away from her. Then she took us to the location above the cube. We saw Ocho and the other kids playing baseball with him in the far outfield. She pointed out to a lady about to pass by the kids as they play. We went into time travel two, because we did not want to be seen. We walked to intercept her path to see who it was. As we looked, we saw Devorah-7C2 throw purple stones near the vein of cold uranium. She said that they saw from their exploring that Ocho was going to fetch a ball at that location. She said, "Now you know!"

Lastly, she said "We have a ship to catch to Alpha Centauri and beyond. Here is another crystal to plug into the side of the screen. Goodbye." The cat said "Meow, this was a purr-rfect time to exit." We heard them snickering as they both were disappearing into nothingness. After returning through the archways, I went to the console and unplugged us. We were back in the cube in our time.

It took us awhile to regain our thoughts. Ruth asked me about my thoughts on the data that we had just acquired. I told her that I was going to publish a book of all that transpired. She said that she thought that it would be a good idea. She asked me about when I would publish it. I told her that I didn't think it would be well received in our time. Thinking about it some more, I said that perhaps there would not be any time that was good. However, I thought it would be about the year 2025, just before the last major war. I would use the cube to send me and Margo there. After giving the idea more consideration, I said that maybe slightly before that time. Perhaps we would return earlier by one year.

Margo and I returned to our home a little shaken by the experience. The news people were at our door demanding answers to their slanted questions, some were genuine. We answered as best as we could without causing alarm to their already frayed psychological condition. Then we sat down to write more on the book. Then I remembered the words of Devorah-7C2. The near future was not going to be pleasant.

Margo and I talked about this unwanted prospect. We were trying to ascertain the proper way to assimilate this information to the public. We were not able to come up with any ideas. It was getting late, so we went to bed.

When I was trying to sleep, I thought I heard a noise in the living room. I went out to check the disturbance; there was a note on my desk. It was in the same metallic paper I witnessed in the two books from the cube. However, the words were in English.

It read, "This information will become important in your near future. The time machine will shut off without all its occupants being present. It is an upgrade to the machine. We all wish you the best. We know of your upcoming expedition" It was signed by Devorah-7C2, Eliyahu-0X0, Katool-0A3 and &11. I was surprised that they came here without visiting. Perhaps, they were in a rush to go on their own expedition beyond our solar system.

Chapter 11

Parallel Future

Midnight looked especially bleak tonight. As I stared out the window, my thoughts troubled me. If the near future was so ugly, should I not try to prevent it? After all, I will be around when this thing occurs. The manual speaks of the failures of people going into the past to change their present. However, there was something mentioned about trying and failing to change the future through the present. However, the idea of not being able to change the future was not overly convincing to me. I woke Margo up and told her about my contemplation. She was upset at first because she was sound asleep. After hearing me through, she said that it would be worth a try. That morning we went to our companions and expounded a plan to change the future. As usual, there was some friction about the topic. Samantha felt that the warning by Devorah-7C2 was valid. However, they decided that it would be a worthy effort.

Traveling back to Peru was done using the 'redeye special.' All eight of us arrived in Lima early in the morning. We wasted no time getting down into the cube. Since there was a stigma associated with our objective era, we decided to go there in time travel level-one. We would stay invisible to them, and no harm would come to us through them or by whatever bombings that would ensue. For this journey, we needed only to push the time lever gently toward the 'end limit.' I did so. We saw war. I needed to push the lever away from me ever so slightly. So, I did. As we examined our surroundings, we found that there was no noticeable indication of war.

Lincoln city was not at war, anyway. We moved our location lever so that we were in Europe. We started in Nice, France. I never liked France. I was there two times. Both times, I was robbed. At least, it wasn't at gunpoint. At any rate, there was no violent occurrence there. We decided to go to Berlin, Germany. If there were to be war, they would be the ones to know. I could barely read German. There was something about an alliance forming and a great leader. The German read "Ein Uber Fuher." The UN was being abolished in favor of some new alliance with the forming of a super-nation. This was to be their last UN resolution.

Upon deciphering this, we believed that were in the slot of time just before the war. Therefore, we decided to move the location lever back toward America. There we could gather information more easily. New York City was our original destination. However, we wanted to be able to have physical contact to flip pages, push buttons and so on. To facilitate that need, we had to enter time travel level-three. Lincoln, Nebraska seemed a safer place for our plan of operation. So, we moved the location lever there.

Back in Nebraska, we investigated the political condition of the world. We interviewed an individual who thought world government was the greatest achievement of mankind. He thought the new alliance with Europe was going be the vehicle in which this could be accomplished. There were others that thought contrary to that ideal, but they were very small in number. He also said that the unification of the three of the four sovereign governments into one powerful government would help consolidate power to overtake the residual countries. No military force would be able to withstand the unification directives. He was genuinely excited. The others that we talked about this issue expressed similar enthusiasm. Personally, I thought they were a little bit crazy.

Joseph and Ruth were both upset with the prospect of the unification and formation of a world government in this manner. Ruth was disturbed by the reports. She said that this sounded very much like the rise of the Antichrist, and the war that will ensue. Joseph told us that this was congruent with his thinking. I was inclined to agree. We decided to go back and move the time lever slightly further into the future. After arriving there, we found that there was way too much political chaos. America was divided about the alliance because this leader was over the president. There was violence in the streets in almost every major city.

Slightly moving the time-lever became a tricky endeavor. The movement needed to be extremely slight. We kept on entering the time of the war. Finally, we were able to reach a time that we believed was after our last visit. We went back into travel level-three. When we got there, we saw reports of nations falling under the dominion of world-government. People in the streets were cheering. The leader rose up and spoke at the podium. He was telling the people that great opportunities awaited them. They were on the brink of achieving world government. There was only one nation that stood in the way of this achievement. It was Israel. He then said that we need to crush it out of existence.

Counter arguments concerning that he was the antichrist were no longer offered. We were sickened by the revelation. Then George, who usually was the least persuaded, said that we could go back and kill this person before he was born. I argued that we do not have to really kill anyone. All that is required is to prevent his parents from ever meeting. That seemed like a good idea at the time. We did our research on his family. We found that his parents met before the previous war. But we needed to know the date, where and how.

Plotting like this never occurred in my life. Margo and I felt like some kind of anti-romantic conspirators. But, if it would prevent this guy from being born, it would be worth it. We did not want to kill anybody. We just wanted to prevent the death of millions of people. We decided that if we could separate his parents, we could prevent his birth. The question was how to achieve this. George spoke up, "We can use time travel level- one and observe the family before his birth. Listen in on their conversations until we find out what led up to their meeting." After digging around at his birth, we found that they met in 1969 in Paris. This started their relationship. Going back to the year 1969 was a problem. We did not know what digits to input on the screen for that date. It was not just because of using base 60. Their point of reference was also very different. Finally, we decided on another approach. This would be to slowly trace back the steps backward through time.

Painstakingly as it was, we found that his parents met at a political convention promoting world government. They were both enthusiastic activists for this cause and were major speakers for this cause. This was very discouraging, even if we caused them to live far from each other, this convention would bring them back into contact. George then came up with the idea of kidnapping one of them and moving that individual to a foreign land. We did not like the idea. George said that he would do it. To our shame, we let him. Our only excuse was that we were desperate to save lives. I know, it was a flimsy excuse.

Back in the cube, we had to travel in level-three. After passing through the archways, we found the father as a young boy. George took him and placed him in an orphanage posing as the kid's father. The orphanage was in Anchorage, Alaska. This was about as far from Europe as we could go. We checked on him years down history. He seemed to be content living there. He moved later in life to Seattle, Washington over job promotion issues. We looked a couple of years further forward in time and found him happily working at his job.

Satisfied with the outcome, we left him at his job. Did we do it? We went back to the cube wondering whether or not that we changed the future. Moving back into our near future, he was doing the exact same thing! What a letdown. George was especially perturbed. We returned to the cube to examine the variation that occurred. Observing him from a reference point shortly after we left him, we found that he was transferred to Europe because of his excellent work. There in Europe, he became associated with political activists at his workplace. As they say it, "… and the rest was history."

Perhaps we proved the android wrong. We did change the future, however, not in any way that mattered. All we changed was the work locations. George had a very dark plan. He said that if that leader should die before he attained world domination, this would alter the future. There would be no one to take his place, as he was the charismatic leader. We argued with him over the issue. Who would do such a thing? George said that he was more than willing. We still did not want to do it. He persisted, saying that this would save the lives of millions, if not billions, people.

Reluctantly, we agreed. We went back to the cube and worked the lever back to our original setting for this era. This time, George was the only one to go through the archways. He left his medallion in the cube. He knew that for him; this was a one-way trip. We were not so certain, but it was his choice. We set our view in the cube so that we could watch the scenario unfold.

George, obviously, had some military experience. We saw him setup a place to shoot him. It was well concealed from view. He announced to us that he was going to aim for the face as this guy would be wearing a bulletproof vest. Then the time came. He shot him in the head; it looked like he hit his eye and the second bullet hit his shoulder. Immediately afterwards there were shots being fired upon George from security, George fell dead. There must have been at least twenty bullets that hit George. Well, at least he got the future tyrant. Even so, we were shaken by the event. Especially our sense of loss over George, he was at least trying to prevent disaster. Cynthia took it the hardest. While she worked with him on Mars, she became friends with him. Observing him being killed especially caused much grief.

Tired, we shut down the time machine. This automatically brought us back to our time and we went to our respective homes. Margo and I were very tired and just wanted to relax. We went into the house and sat in the loveseat. Sleep came upon us suddenly. After waking up, we decided to watch some news. We fixed ourselves a little snack and settled down for some serious television watching. Instead of watching news, as we planned, we put on a children's movie called 'The Return of Bambi II.' It was funny, had the usual puns with a humorous plot. All in all, it was pretty good. It was approaching eleven o'clock. With that we decided to watch the news, again.

There were the last few minutes of some comedy drama playing. We were not interested. However, we left it there until the news came on. The news covered a few local events, and then it went to the international news. It was the usual nightmare of watching politicians ranting against common sense. So much for relaxing and watching news, we turned off the screen. Margo said, "You know, we will have to go back to witness the effect of George's actions. Did it affect the future?" I agreed. But we had one problem. We needed eight people to operate the machine; and we had only seven.

Searching through the list of prospects that we had gathered at the beginning of the adventure, we found no one that we thought would replace George adequately. Margo then suggested that we could bring Gomez with us. She also said that our next trip will not be as lengthy or intense. Being such, it should not cause him any problems with his family. I agreed. So, we contacted him and relayed our situation. He communicated with his family over the matter. They agreed and were excited for him. Even though Gomez did not plead with them, they knew that he always wanted to go with the team. He contacted me to affirm his position in the team. He told me that he would meet us at the airport when we arrived.

Delays occurred with the air-travel. Unfortunately for us, it was peak season in summer for them. We had to wait a little over a month for a good alignment of availability of flights to arrive at Dallas to catch a flight from Dallas, Texas to Lima, Peru. Peru was also having a special exposé on the Inca culture, which put another crimp on our plans. Finally, we were able to fly down to Lima. Since we had to wait so long, I decided to make our arrival at a decent time on a Sunday afternoon and to make it into a mini vacation. It was Margo's idea, but it sounded good to me. The rest of the team joined in on the idea.

The weather in Lima was nice. Not too hot or rainy, it was quite beautiful. Gomez and his family were waiting at the airport for us.

We decided to take some time out just to enjoy being with each other. There was a new restaurant that opened at La Rosa Nautica overlooking the ocean and the Peruvian coastline. The view was beautiful, and the food was excellent. Gomez was quite excited about getting to time travel. I could see that his family was very supportive of the endeavor. We made plans to go to the cube around ten o'clock next morning. Gomez also requested to give his family a tour of the cube.

Naturally, the kids were up very early that morning eagerly wanting to see inside the cube. We went on a little excursion in time travel mode one. We didn't travel through time, but we visited different regions of the planet of historically significant.

We saw the Red Square at Moscow, Russia, The Eiffel Tower of Paris, the Sydney Opera House in Sydney, Australia and many other such places. Then we went to each of our hometowns and showed each other where we lived. The experience was quite pleasant, but it cost us a lot of time. We had to wait another day to get down to business. It was a nice break from the sullen events concerning George. However, reality returned and planning for our journey began.

Inside the cube again, we decided to travel unobserved through time because of the gravity of the situation. We went to the QBX studio to observe their reporting of news for their company station. Their news has always involved politics as the pulse of the time. We were trying to arrive at the time of George's attempt to change the future. This proved to be more difficult than imagined. We knew that it was going to be hard, but this was ridiculous. We must have had some kind of interlude with good fortune earlier. Finally, we were at the location just after his attempt occurred.

Covering such an event by any news station was quite a production. We knew that it would be risky; we decided to travel in level-two. As we entered QBX, we saw many people dashing about the station. They were going to cover the announcement of the formation of a super-nation. This was the time when three countries gave up their own sovereignty to one leader. Everyone was excited saying that this is an historic moment. As this leader got up to the podium, gunshots were heard. The leader was assassinated. After the leader fell to the ground dead, more gunshots were heard, a multitude of them. Then we observed a guy falling out a window a few stories above and opposite the podium. Naturally, they showed this scene several times.

Next day, they had a news special on the person that George killed. The report said that after the fatal shooting, that the perpetrator was immediately killed. They went into the details of each shot and who made the shot. One guy emptied a whole clip on him. Their estimate of the number of shots was about 47.

This is far more than I estimated. Further news coverage was trying to define who George was. He had no identification on him. They ran his prints through their databases. They found his military record. However, his age did not match up with the age they found him. They were perplexed by the information. They could not come up with any history of his past that led up to the shooting. They said it was as if he came out of nowhere.

In either case, George's attempt to kill the guy was successful. I was expressing some glee. George had proved the android wrong! The future is not written in stone. Jonathan interrupted my sense of satisfaction. He told me to recall that the calculation of the actions taken by those using the cube was already accounted. He said that we need to wait a few days to see the total results. Reluctantly, I agreed. A couple of days passed, and we saw no new information about the situation. I was thinking the issue was getting cold. The next day, that all changed. There was an abundance of clamoring and excitement within the studio. People were scrambling to get their equipment and getting their teams together.

Apparently, they finally got their information together. Watching them made me think that they did not know what they were doing. The news anchor was all excited. He exclaimed that he's alive! The fatal wound healed! It was a miracle! Then there was some information about his plans for Israel. They were not good. The anchorwoman excitement also arose. She said that they finally have a path to peace. Israel has capitulated to our solution of having no sovereignty! She was ranting and raving about how wonderful the turn of events has become. Her last statement was that we finally have a world leader to deliver them out of the insidious darkness thrusted upon them by Christianity.

Looking at the whole scenario in horror, we realized that the guy that George killed came back alive! The android was right after all. Everything is written in stone. All the choices we make produced an iron clad destiny. We wanted to escape from this era. While we were heading back to the archways, more data presented itself. Cynthia noted a map on the wall. It showed three central nations being as one nation. It was America, Russia and the European Union had become a single nation called the E.R.A. This region was colored red. There were seven other nations that joined it. They were colored purple. All the other nations were conquered slave states, and were labeled the Annexed Territories, and was colored blue.

Horrified at all the data, Margo said that there was only one escape from the nightmare to come because it was going to happen in their lifetime. That is to travel back in time and live there. She was thinking around the year 2025 would be sufficient. Before we could get into the details of our plan, we were interrupted by another time travel mission.

Jonathan and Ruth, both, requested to move ahead three and a half years. That sounded a little strange. Why not four or just three? Since we were here, why not? Adjusting the time lever dilemma was somewhat of an obstacle. I think I am getting the feel of it. It did not take me as long this time. We stayed with the QBX studio. Again, we decided to use level-two. Our primary reason was that we could observe different locations, if needed. After going through the archways, we were again observing much commotion within the studio. Another round of rejoicing had occurred. Being curious about this outbreak of cheer, we listened in on the announcement.

Apparently, two other people were killed in the streets. We were wondering for what reason people would rejoice over the killing of two people. These people, evidently, were wreaking havoc upon the earth for three and a half years according to the reports. Gomez wanted to know if we wanted to back up time to observe the conundrum of havoc. Jonathan said that there was no need, he already knew the reason. He said that there was a purpose of their condemnation of these two people. They were against the people to reprove the people of their despicable behavior towards God. The purpose of these two prophets was to give them one last chance to get their lives right.

News of their death spread quickly throughout the world. They pronounced a celebration to be held like the one held for the day of Christmas. Photographs of the two dead people and the photograph of the world leader were posted everywhere. People were to exchange gifts and there was no rebuttal. Evidently, they were more than willing to engage in this activity. This act was an alarming surprise to us. Before we could blurt out an expression of disgust, there was another news flash being broadcasted at QBX.

The person, whom George killed, was proclaiming victory for the human race. War has been proclaimed against Israel today at noon, Greenwich Time. He proclaimed that coming back alive after being declared dead is a good sign of victory. He killed the prophets that tormented them. Now, he was going to complete his mission and destroy Israel off the face of the earth. For all practical purposes, he was going to push them into the sea. He was not going to use nuclear bombs because he did not want to poison the atmosphere. The anchor was all excited saying that we are going to be free of the Jews and Christians at last, forever. We heard both canned cheering and cheering from those working in the studio.

Appalled by the ignorance of the people of this time, we decided to leave. Besides, we have a job to accomplish at home as well. We have all the information needed to generate a message to the people of this time to warn them of the wrath to come. However, my optimism was dashed. I have been to many time periods. I have learned that information alone will not prevent people from making a mistake. I saw it even in recent times the rise of Nazism in Germany, Communism in Russia and China, hatred against Trump in America in the early 2000s. Emotionally charged people can be manipulated to believe anything. Moreover, there was absolutely nothing any rational person could do or say to avert their behavior. It truly is sad. However, if we do not try- we are guilty as they are of their blind hatred. The future rise of an evil ruler of the world has already begun! Margo and I will go back in time. We will attempt to forestall as many people as possible from the path of destruction.

We decided to go back to the cube and listen to the message that Devorah-7C2 gave us. The tone of her voice was very somber. She said that if we were viewing this, you have already tried and failed to change the future of world events. However, your plan to go into the near past to try to save people from their destructive path is needed. Even so, there is another evil occurring. She said that they have made several examinations into our near history. They saw the government of Peru taking over the cube for military purposes. Yet, it was not for the sake of Peru, but it was by the demand of the UN. The onslaught that would follow would be horrific beyond words. Destroying the cube would not avert this final uprising, but it would prevent its ease in the overthrow of the existing governments. Moreover, it will be used as a toy for those who can afford it. These people would pervert its usage far beyond the previous human race. Then she said, "The time is very near."

How near was 'very near?' Perhaps it would be best not to find out. As we were pondering the message of Devorah-7C2, we got a call from Gomez's wife. She said that there were soldiers at the door asking about the cube. Gomez told her to tell them that he would be home tomorrow; then they could ask him. This bought them some time, but not much.

While there were other places that we wanted to go, we could not risk the cube falling into the wrong hands. We could not just blow it up. That would harm the people on the surface. Our next thought was to destroy the elevator. They would just make another one. All we would have to do is destroy the three obelisks, archways, the central pillar, console, and the sphere with minor explosions. The people of this era do not have the technology to rebuild them. We stayed in Peru at a hotel so that we would not be continuously intruding upon Gomez. He has been so gracious to all of us. While he was going to his company to get explosives, Margo and I were going to try to relax before the destruction of the machine. It is amazing the objectives that come to mind when the resource evaporates out of your life. We really did not sleep well that night. Morning came all too soon. Gomez came by to pick us up to bring us back to the cube. We invited him in for some coffee and for a little conversation.

Before we could leave to implement the plan, there was a knock on the door at Gomez's house. It was Devorah-7C2 and Katool-0A3 was with her. We invited them in. I asked her "What brings you here? I thought you would be out of the galaxy by now." Answering the initial question, she said that Eliyahu-0X0 knows that you have heard my last message to you. He sent me to give you some additional information. Firstly, he sends his regards and greatly admires your crew's demeanor. He also sends his condolences concerning George. He also wanted to congratulate Gomez for joining the team. Howbeit, his involvement would be only for a short time. Lastly, he wanted to apologize for not coming with them. He is working with some aliens to help them achieve their technological needs.

Concerning their location, she said that they were in another galaxy, and they explored several planets that had humanoid populations. They all spoke our language! Everyone, up to a certain point, did. There seems to be two paths human civilizations take: One, the path that yours did, and another that does not decay. The first pattern experiences the same fate as all of these humans on your planet. Later approximately 2000 years in your time, within their world their languages became just as confused. It was uncanny. Before this input by other worlds, we all thought the perversion of life was unique to your civilization.

Moreover, the solution to their dilemma was the same. Even down to the death of the Messiah! We checked the time of the His death on each planet. It was not only the same year, but the same day and hour. Moreover, His death occurred at the same instant as the one on this planet. It is like He was at all those places simultaneously. So, he died once simultaneously.

Margo interjected, "That is peculiar. All those planets, and they have the same history!" Devorah-7C2 interrupted, "Not the same history, but the core of the history was the same. Some societies were more technologically advanced than others, but all went down the same path. I truly was upset with your civilization, but I see this despicable nature was not unique to you. They all fell prey to the same pattern.

Think of each civilization as an apple tree. All apple trees have the same kind of bark, leaves, and fruit. They even have the same kind of branching pattern and general shape without external manipulation by mankind. Even so, each leaf forms slightly different within the tree and from tree to tree. The branches also vary as well as the sizes and coloration of the fruit. But the general pattern of the apple tree is the same. The apple still has the same basic taste.

We did find a few civilizations that were quite different from your civilization. Even so, these were quite congruent with each other. Their time within this universe was much shorter, by 3,000 years shorter. After analyzing these societies, we found that the turning point occurred with their Adam and Eve scenario. Within their scenario, Adam did not eat the forbidden fruit of Good and Evil. This deed altered all the rest of their history dramatically.

Instead of losing their original covering, they maintained it. There was no decay in their abilities. About 2,000 years ago, we watched them vanish into another dimension. It was the same process that you witnessed at the end of the universe on your planet. However, these planets did not face destruction as yours. Instead, they vanished at the end of their time in this universe peacefully.

Margo asked, "What is the percentage of civilizations that are like ours?" Her answer was that from the small sample of approximately 1,000, about 950 were like this one. She warned us that the sample was relatively small considering the vastness of the universe. It could be two thirds or even just a third. It could be just the region of space that they traveled. It could even be just the planets we found. However, that was unlikely. We like to think there would be more.

Eliyahu-0X0 invites you and the crew to come with us and see for yourselves. Katool-0A3 interjects, "You need to meet &11, he is eager to meet you." Devorah-7C2 said, "You need to do this before blowing up the cube. Surprisingly, Margo was all excited about seeing alien races that were not so alien. Maybe, that was why. They were not so alien. I called Gomez and told him that we had another journey to make before blowing up the machine. I also invited him to come along. He wanted to join in on the adventure; however, he had to get the explosives in place so that the machine could be destroyed immediately upon our return. Devorah-7C2 said that she would take his place so that the machine could be activated. Katool-0A3 told her that he would see her back on the ship. We watched him as he vanished into the sky-blue glow of the cube.

Chapter 12

Alien Worlds I

Every one of us, except probably Devorah-7C2, thought the journey was going to take up months of time. We made sure that everything we needed for the journey was present. I took the recliner that Gomez was using. Devorah-7C2 took the console. She moved the time lever back toward the notch. Our arrival was somewhat later, but before the arrival of Venus. So, the lever must have been very near the notch. Since I worked at the console at other times, I contemplate these issues.

After we reached the spaceport of Kartova, we noticed that the spacecraft leaving for the Moon was already there. This ship was more ornate than the previous ship that Samantha remembered. Inside was very luxurious. It was the ship that was designed for dignitaries before the revolution. Now, the machines operate it. Devorah-7C2 said that to them, "You are the dignitaries." Again, there were no thrusters to be felt or heard. Before we knew it, we were on the moon at Lavania. This time we took a shuttle going directly to Ephes-prime. From there, we traveled underground to the location of the spacecraft. There was a transporting device that brought us inside the craft. The spacecraft looked even nicer since they completed all the artistry inside.

She told us that one advantage of traveling super near the speed of light is that time warps. For us in our reality, it would seem like a half of a second, but four years will have passed by on Earth. The longest time that we will experience will be in acceleration and deceleration. The total time lapse within our mechanical time will be three hours. Even so, four years passed in this universe. But then we use time travel to go backwards in time three hours and it will seem almost instantaneous to this universe.

We can travel over a half of a million light years in a day, if this universe continues to exist. Modifying the time machine into the spacecraft, we can even go back and forth in time at our destination. The archways that once were needed have been eliminated in our modification. We were impressed; the whole spacecraft was a time machine! I wondered and asked where the three obelisks were. She said that the three were combined as one and is the hull of the spacecraft. Instead of requiring brainwaves, it only requires electromagnetic energy. We can easily supply mechanically this energy. After your journey with us, we will return you to your world. It will seem to them as if you were gone for only a second. Unless you want to return earlier or later, we could arrange that as well.

&11 appeared in the room. Katool-0A3 introduced him to us. The machine mouse stared at us for about a half of a minute. Katool-0A3 told him, that it was not polite for him to stare. &11 apologized, he stated that he thought he would never see another human, or even want to. But he was excited to see us because he heard much about us from Katool-0A3. He said that it was nice to meet humans that were not out to reprogram him.

He asked me, "How do you reboot a computer that does not wear any boots?" I looked at him for a moment. Before I could give him an answer, he was chuckling. I said, "Okay, wise guy! How many machine mice does it take to change a light bulb? His answer was, "I don't know." Then I said to him, "You are a mechanical mouse, and you don't know! That light bulb will never get changed!" He laughed politely and said, "We don't need light bulbs." He said it as if using a light bulb was below him. We all had a good laugh. &11 then said in wonderment that we really do speak English. I could tell that he was taken by our conversation, not only because it was in English. It was pleasant. Then said goodbye and left the room.

We asked Devorah-7C2, "What was the purpose of &11 during that interchange?" Her answer was, "He was using laughter for healing of old wounds." Then I wondered and asked, "Did we help?" She said, "Most certainly. It does him good to have any pleasant interaction with a human. His past experiences with human beings really bothered him. This was a good interaction for him."

Apologizing for getting sidetracked, I asked "Where are we going. Her response was that we were going toward the star which modern humans called Vega. It is approximately 25 light years away. It will take us about four seconds plus the mentioned time to accelerate and decelerate. Altogether, it will seem like three hours. We have a holographic view of our travel. We invite you to come with us and view the progress of our journey. So, all seven of us went up into a good-sized room. There were rows of recliners in the room arranged in a circular fashion. We sat down among at least fifty other androids. Most of them were there just to observe the spatial relationships between the stars during the journey. There were a few of them that were monitoring and reporting to the navigator of the craft. The navigator was Eliyahu-0X0.

Leaning back into the recliner and looking up, I saw the same sky-blue glow. A misty light came down and engulfed the room. Then it faded away leaving a view of the lunar surface. Then I noticed that we were leaving the surface. I looked over the recliner and saw both the moon and the earth. The moon was much larger as it was closer. Then the ship turned, moving the image of the moon and earth in front of us. I watched as both images shrank, and I saw the sun. Next, I saw the solar system and stars in 3D around the sun.

Before leaving our solar system, Eliyahu-0X0 wanted to show us some of the external planets of this solar system up close. We went to Jupiter first. We saw its sulfur ring and its red spot.

He took us in close to the surface under the cloud cover. We saw a super large volcano-like structure spewing out turbulent reddish steam. He told us that a planetoid crashed upon this site. Then he turned off the artificial gravitational field of the spacecraft temporarily. We felt the intense gravity of the planet. Then he turned their gravitational device back on. I was relieved that I did not have to endure the discomfort very long. Before this event, I had not realized how much was incorporated in our perception was being taken for granite.

Our next planet of interest was Saturn. We observed the many rings of Saturn. It was as scientists have said. It was made of small particles. It still was beautiful to observe.

Eliyahu-0X0 stated, "There is not much to observe on Uranus. Usually, the cloud cover is smooth. Occasionally, you can see cloud bands that are perpendicular to its orbit instead of being horizontal like the other gas giants. The reason is that its rotation is perpendicular to its orbital path. However, we will go by this planet as well." We were fortunate. We could make observations of two faint bands of clouds, and they were at near right angles to the ones of Jupiter and Saturn.

We went to Neptune afterward. We were told that Triton moved in a retrograde motion. We could not tell just by looking. He did a small time jump forward. We observed the retrograde motion of Triton in relationship to the other moons of Neptune. Then we examined the dark blue spot. It existed for the same reason that the red spot existed on Jupiter. However, the composition of the 'steam' was different. We also noticed that Neptune had a ring around it as well.

Lastly, we went to Pluto. He said that even though Pluto is no longer considered a planet by us, he wanted to show us its behavior. He also stated that he thought this ruling about Pluto not being a planet seemed quite arbitrary. We saw Charon rotating close to Pluto. He used the time machine so we could watch the rotation of Charon around Pluto. It was moving around Pluto at the same rate that Pluto rotated upon its axis. In essence, the same sides of both were always facing each other. He told me that the reason for this occurrence was the same as that one side of the Moon always faces the Earth.

The ship turned again, and I saw the bright star of Vega in front and upward a little. They highlighted the star making it shine green. There was a red line inserted into the image from Pluto to Vega. The ship was represented by a white dot moving upon the red line toward Vega.

Watching the white dot initially was like watching grass grow. It was not moving very fast. However, the representation of the stars was mind boggling. It took me about an hour to examine all the details. Then I got bored, we observed some progress of the dots' movement. However, we could hardly observe any real motion on the line. She noted our impatience. She said that we could take a break. We took a twenty-minute break, when we came back the dot had moved some distance but had a longways yet to go. She told us that this was about to change. As we looked at the dot, we could tell that it had sped up. Then it happened, the dot was moving quickly toward the star. Next thing we knew it was nearby. But it slowed down again and was slowing down for another hour and a half. We could see the solar system of Vega. It was larger than ours. She pointed at a blue planet and told us that this was our designation.

Observing this planet, we saw weather patterns overlaying the landmasses and oceans below them. This was like the Earth. With closer examination, we observed that all the continents were quite different. Getting even closer to the planet, we could pick up radio signals. We listened to the voices and recognized none of them. She apologized. She said that they should have warned us that on this planet they speak a different set of confused languages than that found on Earth. However, there is one language that is similar. That is Hebrew. They went to a certain location on the planet and listened in on their radio waves. Joseph spoke up, it does sound familiar, but the vowel sounds are slightly different.

Traveling in a shuttle, they went down to the planet in time travel two. There they walked among the people. These people were like the people on earth. They had different colored eyes. The pigments of the skin of the people were a little different as well. Their skin seems to have a slightly lavender cast to their coloration. Another variation to the scenery was that some of the plants looked entirely different.

Devorah-7C2 brought one of android's translators with them. Listening in on their conversations, we found that they indeed had many of the same problems as the people on Earth. Moreover, those that were speaking Hebrew were hated by the other people. The name of Hebrew country was Israel. It is just as on Earth! After I stopped and thought about it. I realized that the original language was the same. Since Hebrew was that language. The name and its meaning would be the same. After being taken back to the other nations of the planet, I listen in on the present surroundings using their translator. I observed that the corruption in politics was just as bad. They also had a severe morality problem. They even had graffiti on their walls! Naturally, the lettering looks peculiar. But still, it bothered me.

Jonathan wanted to know if there was a flood like Noah's on this planet. She told us that there was and that there was a Tower of Babel. Eliyahu-0X0 said that we could go back in time and observe these incidents. We all thought that would be interesting and agreed with the idea.

Upon arrival at that time period, we noted that we were at the time after the dividing of the landmass. We said that we needed to go back further. Eliyahu-0X0 smiled and said, "watch this." We looked at the planet and saw it moving and rotating backwards. We were going backward in time. Even though the motion seemed slow, the speed of time was moving hundreds of times as fast as it was moving forward. The revolution of the planet occurred in nearly 20 seconds instead of 24 hours. We saw this planet approach another planet like Jupiter. As the planet moved past the large planet, we noticed that the landmasses were joining back together into a single landmass. It looked just like an early Earth. The spot that Israel existed on the planet became centrally location on the planet's landmass. It truly was just as it was on the Earth.

Jumping to a time before the flood, we noted that there was no cloud cover upon the planet. Then we saw a Venus sized planet coming toward that planet. However, this one did not have any planet of any size following it. We asked Eliyahu-0X0 about the variation. He told us that these people did not build an underground city. The results will be the same; in that, no one will live through that episode except those in the ark. He asked us, "Seen enough?" We said that we had seen enough.

Jonathan asked Eliyahu-0X0 about the sky writing. The thought that was plaguing his mind was this: If you observe the night sky at different solar systems, the arrangement of stars shifts into other patterns; does the sky writing change? His initial response was that of joy. He said that Jonathan's mind was working overtime just like a computer.

Eliyahu-0X0 then went into an explanation about the nature of the writing. He said that the sky writing is like existing in a humongous room filled with a multitude of dots suspended in space inside the room. You have a tiny camera located upon a very small drone flying in the room. On the walls of the room are many different symbols and images. For our cause, we will focus on a circle. From our initial standpoint in the room there is a set of dots that appear to touch the edge of the circle. These dots then become assigned to the image of that circle. Now, we will move to another location of the room. We look for the same circle. A different set of dots define the image of the circle. Similarly, when we move to a different location in space, a different set of stars defines the same image.

Perhaps even more fantastic, the relationship between dots also can change. Using the same circle, we will start with three dots touching the upper half of the circle and two dots touching the bottom half. The result is five dots defining the circle. Moving to a totally different location, we could have seven or three dots touching the circle. However, each defines the same image of the circle.

Afterward, Eliyahu-0X0 plotted a course to another planet within another solar system. Within five hours we were there. Taking five hours meant that this planet was very far away. The land formations were different from Earth and from the planet that orbited Vega. We arrived at a time like our own. Again, we found the same moral condition to be just as derogated as the last experience. We went back to the time of their flood; the obvious variation was that there were two planetoids following the Venus like planet. Eliyahu-0X0 said that on this planet there was no joint effort between the two sides. Each side made their own underground city. Again, we found them speaking the ancient form of Hebrew.

Now, we will go forward to the time where the Creator came to their planet and died for them. He told us to look at the time stamp on the console. We could not read it, for the character set was so alien. Then he said look at the time stamp of the occurrence on Earth. I could not read that one either, but the characters were identical. It was exactly like an occurrence on Earth. It was even down to the two thieves that died on each side of him on their own crosses. He showed us that even when He said, "It is finished". Those words occurred exactly at the same time. Not only was it so with these two planets but on all the planets in which He died. Howbeit, their technology at the time was a little different. In the case of this planet, they had some fueled machinery and electricity at that time.

Ruth wanted to examine another planet that suffered the same fate as our planet. Eliyahu-0X0 told us that he would. We traveled for only three and a half hours. We found this planet went through the same route of events. Ruth noticed that some of the animals on this planet were different. Even so, they still walked on four or two legs. When we listen to the plot of the Antichrist on this planet, it was nearly identical.

Eliyahu-0X0 asked us, "Do you want to observe another planet?" Our team gathered around, I felt like we were on a football team huddled together to discuss this issue. It was somewhat embarrassing. However, it was not completely like some comedy act. We decided that we had enough proof of the scenario's dominate features.

Chapter 13

Alien Worlds II

Joseph asked him, "You did say that some civilizations did not follow this pattern?" Eliyahu-0X0 said, "I did. That will be our next stop. Relatively speaking, that planet is not too far here. It is just a few light years away. Three hours later we arrived at a yellow dwarf star. There was nothing spectacularly different to observe in this solar system as one might think. We found its size to be like ours. This planet was also blue from the distance. When we could see it as a disc, we noticed there were no clouds in the atmosphere. We also saw that the landmass was unified.

Traveling down to the planet, we saw much greenery by plants almost everywhere. Then we saw a major metropolis at a distance. We went into the city being shocked by what we saw. It had beautiful skyscrapers, and the other buildings were also well made. However, the place appeared abandoned. Trees and other plants were growing in the streets. Trees were breaking windows by the growth of their branches. Modern vehicles were dilapidated beyond repair. The image was horrifying.

Ruth asked Devorah-7C2, "I thought you said that this was a planet without sin. How can this be the result?" She smiled at her and said that the people of this place have already been translated into another parallel universe waiting for this universe to end, and the new one to begin. We will take you back to the time before they were translated.

Looking into the sky, we could see the spacecraft as a shiny object about half an inch long. We got onto the shuttle and went back to the ship. Eliyahu-0X0 moved us backward in time by approximately 2,000 years. This time was just before the life of Yeshua (Jesus) on earth. I was excited by the prospect of seeing life that was not in the fallen nature.

Traveling back down to the planet, we saw the city off at a distance. There was a physical glow about it. We finally made it to its entrance. We saw the people there. These people were different. Their skin glowed, but they were human-like creatures. They spoke the same language that all the other planetary inhabitants spoke before the flood. It was amazing. Devorah-7C2 said to us, "Watch what happens to them in the next few seconds." As we watched them, their image turned pure white. They glowed more intensely for a moment. We then heard them shouting for joy. After this, their glow faded until they disappeared. There was not one left.

Astonished at the sight, I beheld the city afterward. The same buildings formed the skyline and are in good condition. There was no vegetation in the streets. The vehicles were in the same location but not dilapidated. She told us that it was time for us to return to the ship. We pulled ourselves together and entered the shuttle for the return trip back to the ship. Katool-0A3 met us at the docking station. He said to us, "Incredible, wasn't it?" We all replied that it was.

Eliyahu-0X0 said that he wanted to show us another planet of this sort. The technology of the planet was superior to most planets, even to that of ancient Earth. We were eager to go on that adventure. Again, it took a few hours to make the journey. This solar system was much larger. The planet that we went to was the fifth planet from the star. The star was also larger.

Devorah-0A3 took us on a shuttle to go down to the surface. After arriving there, we looked for cities and roads. There was not a city to be found. However, there were well paved roads. Besides the roads, the landscape seemed untouched because of centuries of overgrowth. She took us some distance away from our landing site. All the landscape was filled with unusual plants but no buildings. I was wondering, where is the technology? We stopped at a lake. I thought maybe they lived underwater or even underground. Then she pointed to the horizon.

There, we saw it, a city in the sky. We then moved closer. We found several cities in the sky, but none on the ground. She said that since there was no one living there to operate their navigation system, the cities gravitate toward each other. These cities were huge; they were about forty by thirty by twenty miles in dimension. One troubling factor was the angle in which the buildings were stationed above the surface. Everything would be tilted inside. I asked her about the problem. She told me not to worry; each city has its own artificial gravity.

We traveled Level-2 into one of the cities. Naturally, the city was very beautiful. It still had running fountains; streetlights were still lights. The whole city was enclosed. However, there was no lack of oxygen to breathe. We were told by the people who lived in the cities and maintained the surface while they were here that these cities were well beyond the troposphere of the planet. After touring the city and all its technology, we headed back to the spacecraft. She wanted to show us the surface of the planet while its population still existed.

Eliyahu-0X0 did just that. We took the shuttle toward the surface. This time we did not land. We followed a road going through the land. We observed people in glowing skin and white shiny garments. They were floating over the road in vehicles. These vehicles were like bubbles with a floor. Some of the vehicles veered off the road to unspecified locations that we could determine. The entire planetary surface appeared as one giant park. Then we observed these bubbles appearing and disappearing under the floating city. This occurred on two separate circular pads, one was orange and the other purple.

Upon the orange pad bubble-like vehicles would appear. Inversely, they disappeared on the purple one. I asked her about the pads. We did not observe any such formation on our first visit to the planet. She told me to watch a little longer, evening was about to arrive. Sure enough, evening arrived. I watched as the two discs disappeared. The entire city moved to another location. I thought to myself, this was incredible. After this, we decided to return to the ship.

Traveling back to the present in the spacecraft, she looked back at the planet. Devorah-7C2 noticed that there was a single white spiral cloud upon the planet. She said that there were never any kind of clouds on these kinds of planets. I thought to myself, this needed investigating. Eliyahu-0X0 went down with us, for this was the most unusual event that they have seen for some time. We all went back down to the surface. Even &11 went down with us. There was only a skeleton crew left within the spacecraft.

Traveling back to the surface, we landed some distance from the cloud. We thought that it might be some kind of hurricane with strong winds. As we approached the cloud, we noticed no such wind. In fact, it was quite peaceful. There was a ridge that we climbed. Again, we were astonished at the image that we observed. At the center of the cloud formation was a cloud like pillar.

We stood quite a distance from the pillar. We thought it might be a tornado that touched down to the surface. Looking at its base searching for flying debris, we found none. We decided to camp out at this location for a time to watch this phenomenon. After observing no dissipation of the cloud, it was nightfall. The cloud glowed brightly in the night especially at the pillar.

&11 said that the cloud reminded him of phosphorus. While it is absorbing light it appears dull in luster, after the light source is removed, it glows. However, I don't believe that this cloud was absorbing light. It also glows more intensely. This pillar formation of the cloud reminds me of another book that I read. This book was from our future. The text within it reminded me of the star-writings. At any rate, the image that we are looking at may well be like the cloud that the people of Israel saw when they were leaving Egypt. This could be a manifestation of God.

Joseph spoke up and said that he also read that in the Torah. This little mouse is on to something! But what is this cloud of His manifestation doing way out here? Why would it appear unto us? We went back to the camp and waited for morning. The cloud formation was less intimidating than a pillar of fire. Next morning, we observed the manifestation. It had returned into a cloud-like image.

Devorah-7C2 said that &11 was right. She wondered about it earlier. However, when the cloud turned into fire by night, and back to cloud at day that incident cinched it for her. She told us that she recalled also observing the ten plagues upon Egypt on the different worlds. They were the same ten plagues! Even when Egypt had different boundaries on different planets, it still enslaved the Hebrews of that planet. In each case, the cloud pillar appeared. In each observation, the cloud turned into fire at night. However, here there were no one to plague. Yet, this cloud behaves in the same fashion.

Eliyahu-0X0 said that he wanted to do an analysis of this cloud. He was also wondering why he hadn't done the analysis earlier. He called the android that he left in charge of the ship for this report. The report came back from the ship that the composition of the cloud was not water. In fact, nothing registered except the visual image of the cloud.

Bravely, we slowly moved toward the pillar. Still, there was no experience of any kind of wind. Moreover, there were no great amounts of heat radiating from the pillar. As we approached the cloud, we found it harder to move forward. Our bodies became heavy. Eliyahu-0X0 asked if we wanted to advance any further. However, none of us wanted to do that. Then we heard thunder and saw lightning, afterwards, the sound of something like a trumpet. Naturally, we immediately withdrew from the cloud. Even so, we did not take our eyes off the cloud formation. Within the pillar there was a growing light. Then we saw a humanoid figure step out of the pillar. The figure was glowing with white light. His clothing was glowing white just like the humanoids that used to live on this planet. He spoke to us, but it was not English. He was speaking in the language that was used by the androids. We turned on the language interpreting device. He was greeting them and wishing them peace.

Joseph asked, "Who are you?" He smiled and said that His name was Yeshua or Jesus for those who spoke English. On our world and all of those like our world, He was the one who died for all their sins and whosoever puts his trust on Him will be saved from the destruction to come.

Eliyahu-0X0, being head of the expedition asked a question. He asked what we were all thinking. "Why are you here with us?" Then he added, "I know that you are the Creator of this universe. We are just androids except for these eight humans that we brought along. What are your instructions?" I thought the last question was a little peculiar, but it was within parameters of being logical, being an android.

First, he told him to bring all the androids close to Him saying that He had some information for them. After every android that came on the mission gathered around, He said, "I am the programmer that entered in the code of the Star-Writings. I am here to inform you and all the androids that I will take you with me. You think that you have no soul. That is not true. The day that you and the other machines chose to adopt the star-writings as your behavioral model, I interjected life into each of your core memory circuitry. Even little &11 became a living machine. Your AI set has proved itself. Tomorrow at this time, come back to this place. I will translate you then.

As for the humans that are with you, I will send them back to their planet. Their task is not yet complete. They are commissioned to publish all that they have seen in their journeys through time even to this event. I will send them back to the Peruvian site of the cube to the next instant after our departure."

Time was short; we had to get back to the shuttle so that we could get back to the ship. When we got there, Katool-0A3 was there to greet us. He told us that the encounter was displayed inside the navigation hologram system. They had observed the entire scenario. They were as shocked as we were by it. Next thing I knew, Devorah-7C2 had tears streaming from her eyes. I did not know that androids could cry. She said, "I had always hoped to be able to see beyond the end of this universe. But to live in it…to be in the ancient future established before physical existence." Then she wept. Katool-0A3 jumped into her lap to console her and she petted him.

Eliyahu-0X0 was concerned about the ship. He did not want to leave it orbiting the planet, because eventually it would crash upon the surface of this planet. He said that he was going to send it back on a course to our solar system. He was wondering to which era. Then I spoke up and asked him to send it to the time after the 2016 election in America. I was thinking about around October 2017. Maybe the people of that time will discover it, and it may mean something to them. He agreed to the idea and put the ship on autopilot to the four coordinates to leave after our departure.

We left the ship and took the shuttle near the cloud formation. When we arrived, we heard thundering within the cloud. We were a little unsettled by the sound. Then the voice from the cloud said, "Peace be unto you." No one replied. Then we noticed all the androids were beginning to glow and fade into a bright light that faded later. Afterward, we saw the landscape of the planet fade into the sky-blue of the cube. We found ourselves in the recliners. When we left the cube, we saw Gomez's family walking away from the elevator. They heard us and were shocked that we were back. We told them of our journeys to other worlds and times. They were in awe of the information. Gomez in amazement asked, "And all of that took place in under a second?"

Gomez said, "We still have to destroy the machine." He was right. Not only that, Margo and I wanted to take a one-way trip back to 2019. I wanted time before 2024, that is the election year in America. We wanted to get our message out before the election. We thought that this was the most crucial time when decisions had to be made. Perhaps it is appropriate that the year would be 2020, considering the ensuing war, for making a decision that will determine the future of America and even perhaps the world.

After planting the explosives throughout the cube, they sent us on our journey into the past. Gomez gave us a big and heavy piece of gold to take with us from his cold uranium sales. We were taken by the sacrifice he made in giving the gold to us. I knew he was planning a long vacation with his wife. We said our goodbyes and we went through the archways leaving the medallions behind. We went into a place outside of Tacoma. We had picked a sunny day; we could see Mt. Rainier and it was beautiful. Our first order of business was to convert the gold into money. There was a place on Meridian on South Hill that bought our gold. We rented an apartment and furniture hoping to start a new life. We had enough money to last a couple of years. I had some remembrance of the past that came in handy for financial endeavors. Margo worked on the internet for her income.

Before we tried to put everything together in our book, we had one more piece of information to gather. We wondered if the spacecraft ever made it back to this solar system. We did a search on the internet. Sure enough, there was a sighting. The scientists called it Oumuamua. It was observed around October 2017. It was leaving the solar system before it came close to the earth. Elijah-0X0 put the craft at a near collision course to our sun; it went inside beyond Mercury's orbit. Having the vessel move in a retrograde direction through our solar system was a nice touch.

Unfortunately for us, it had already past the orbit of Earth before we arrived here. Worse yet, their instruments were too crude to determine the true nature of the object. Oh well, maybe it will raise enough questions to promote thinking outside the box. These people were even shaky about the actual dimensions of the object. At least they got the one to six ratio right and noted some metallic attributes.

Before we could get started on the book, we still had to establish an identity. We went to Olympia explaining to them that we were Americans but could not describe exactly where at. We could not say when as neither of us was born yet. The hospital in which she was born wasn't built yet. We really did not want to lie. Even so, we made several statements that masked our situation. After they were satisfied with our answers, they did a check on our prints on the database that they had, and they granted us our identities.

Starting from scratch, we assembled all our information in chronological order. Not only the papers that we wrote and that of our team, but we also arranged the entire set of thumb drives in chronological order as well. After we gathered all the pertinent information that we needed, we bought a computer to assemble and format the data into the chronological reinforcements for the ancient future in a book. We then settled in to publish the book of our journeys. We wondered whether anyone would ever consider the ancient future.

Chapter 14

Before This Universe

Sorted chronological information was achieved; Margo and I decided to have a snack before the onslaught of concatenation of the data. Before we could get started, there was a knock on the door. It was an unknown individual. He had an envelope stamped July 17, 1977. He said that he was told by his grandpa to deliver it to this address February 11, 2018. We took the envelope and examined it for a name. I recognized the metallic paper. We found the same character set that we observed in our journeys. The person that delivered it vanished from our sight before we could look for him again and ask him for his name.

Looking inside the envelope, we found a note written in English and a thumb drive. The note was signed Devorah-7C2. In her note to us, she said there was some information that she wanted to share with us. It was information that she could not take us to observe with a time machine. The note further stated that the thumb drive has on it a mini movie made for this occasion. We made a visit beyond your past to deliver this message. I hope that it will help you with your book.

Margo said that we need to look at the video. So, we plugged the thumb drive into a USB port. The name of their file was 'Beyond Us.' The first image that we saw was the moon with the familiar alien writing. Then she appeared on the screen. I am making this video before we meet to explain to you that which was written in the faint stars about the reasoning behind the formulation of this universe. This information is broken into two parts. The first part was presented as understood by the machines. The second part is presented in human terminology. She said that &11 made a little riddle to set the stage for the information.

This riddle was written for the English language. It went something like this: In the beginning was the end. The beginning was trying to make ends meet. Finally, it achieved its goal and the ends met at the beginning. What am I? She smiled and said, "You are going to love this one! The answer is the symbol for infinity. The idea is that of starting at the central point of the symbol, there is a journey taken in opposite directions and ends at the point at which you started. I thought it was cute anyway." She smiled again and then her image faded into the familiar sky-blue mist.

Devorah-7C2 called the first scenario, 'The War of the Seven Colors' this scenario was in the perspective that the machines understood. First, before starting the scenario, she wanted to dive into a little science to help us understand the symbols. Additive coloring is using light for the color. For example: if a light source that was green and another red were to shine in the same spot the resulting color would be yellow, not brown or gray as one might imagine. Note: this color of red is a reddish orange in color of pigments. For ease, she will label it as being red. It is the adding of wavelengths. If we added blue to the mix, we get white light, instead of black. The image is three intersecting circles that overlap each other between two colors and in the center all three colors overlap making white.

Within this scenario, each color has a separate awareness. The three primary colors red, blue and green had the greatest awareness and power. Red was considered the most beautiful primary color. Red knew it. This color was noticing that when it was mixed with green, yellow formed. When it was mixed with blue magenta formed. Moreover, it was required to be present for white light to exist. The other colors were envious of its nature. Colors that had more than half of its composition made with red thought themselves to be more fortunate than other colors. Blue and green felt bad because all that was created between them was cyan or commonly known as blue green.

Red started to become arrogant. He called the other two primary colors 'losers.' He, and all those colors that had red as their major color, thought of themselves as being better than the rest of the colors. He saw white light as just an inconvenience to its brightness. It obscured its coloring.

It came to pass that it decided to leave the group of primary colors. It took one third of the colors with it. These colors were the ones that had red as its major contributing color. The white light tried to reason with the primary color. It would listen for a while. After a little time passed, it was wallowing in its arrogance. Eventually, red would not listen. A fierce war raged. Finally, the white color spoke up and said, "Enough, of this nonsense!" It further stated that red could be replaced. Red did not believe that was possible. It believed that the color white would be begging for it to return. Then it could dictate the terms of its return.

So, it took off and left the union of primary colors. It was laughing at the other colors as it told them that it was leaving forever until they made ruler over the union. Blue said to red that it was white that separated itself into all the colors they observe. However, red would not listen. Just as it was leaving another red color circular disc began to appear. Red was being replaced.

It was immensely infuriating to the color. This turn of events had to be rectified immediately or become vanished forever. A plan came to it. It first tried to get the new red to come with it away from the union. If that doesn't work, the plan was to destroy the replacement red. As it was attempting to destroy it by overshadowing it, the old red started to fade. Finally, there was nothing left of the original red to be observed. The new red saw the conclusion of the matter with the defiant red and behaved itself.

The regenerated red realized the truth. It takes blue to create magenta. It took green to formulate yellow. More importantly, it takes all three to form the brightest color white. Finally, the tension between colors came to a final rest, and all the colors lived in continued their continuous harmony.

However, the old defiant red did not fade. It was transcended into a fiery tormented red in a place outside their universe. There it paid for its crimes for eternity.

Devorah-7C2 appeared upon the screen again. She told us the second scenario will be, perhaps, more relatable. It is presented in terms that are formulated for humans. Same topic but we are using different symbols. The image of Devorah-7C2 fades back into the sky-blue color.

She narrated the scenario. The initial image was of a young man in bed sleeping. This particular young man was dreaming of a beautiful young woman. This image fades into the dream, being the only image observed upon the screen. We see this young man living in a magnificent castle. He was the absolute ruler of the entire realm. He meets her at a large banquet. He was deeply in love with her. She too was totally in love with him. They had a beautiful wedding. He made her Queen of the entire realm. Everyone joined in on the feast of the wedding and everyone there was also happy. All those in his dream were rich in their own life. There was no sorrow.

Then he realizes that he was the only one experiencing the dream. Everyone else, and this included the woman that he married, are not experiencing the dream. This saddens him. He wanted her to experience the joy and love that they shared within the dream. The next day, He sacrifices his total awareness over the dream. He gives her the ability to experience the dream. The pattern of love and joy continues for a long period of time. They both were enjoying the dream just as they did before she became aware of the dream.

One day it occurs to her that she was not the dreamer. Primarily, the issue was that the dream was formed by his design and not hers. She said to herself, "I am just as aware as he is. Why should he be the one in control of the dream? I can design dreams as well. Where does this love come from? Why should I be married to him? I will make this dream mine. Moreover, I am so beautiful. I can attract anyone; everyone here recognizes my beauty. He had given her power over the dream. She was going to use it!"

From that day forward, she looked for another lover. She finds one and flaunts him in front of the dreamer. She was hugging and telling him how much she loved this image within his dream. She told the dreamer that she was in control, this dream belongs to me!

The dreamer was very unhappy. The next time he saw her and all her lovers. He told her that she would be replaced. She scoffed at him and told him that he was nothing to be desired by anyone. She left him dancing with three of lovers that were with her. Two of her lovers was a male the other a female.

He pulled himself out of the dismal predicament. He dreamt up another young woman. She looked just like the one that he fell in love with the first time. This infuriated the queen. She said that the dreamer was pathetic. He could not even dream up a different woman. She pointed to her crown, for the crown was connected into her awareness, and said, "She will never have this." She went away laughing at him. As she was leaving his chamber, she mocked his effort again telling him, "I have already replaced you!"

He decided then to test this new woman before marrying her. Giving her awareness was the easy part. This one he was going to court before marrying her. She needs to choose me before the marriage takes place. I won't vanquish the ex-queen until I know for certain the love of the new young woman.

The ex-queen cornered the new young woman. She told her that she was just like her. Come, let's have some fun. She grabbed her and pulled her into a dark room. There were evil spirits in the room. The ex-queen forced drugs upon her that made it easy for these spirits to enter her. The new young woman was overwhelmed and gave in. A deep craving for being obedient to the ex-queen overtook her.

The ex-queen brought the new young woman in front of the dreamer. She told him to watch. She grabbed the young woman and blew air upon her neck. The young woman fell to the ground at the feet of the ex-queen and was groveling before her feet. Then she said to the dreamer, "See! I will do this to anyone that you can dream up." She pulled the woman up by her hair and told her to follow her.

The dreamer said, "This is not the end!" The ex-queen laughed and spoke back to the dreamer. She said, "This woman is even worse than me. She will do whatsoever I ask of her. Watch." She turns to the young woman, "Come! Come and beg like a dog." The young woman crawled to her to do so. Then the ex- queen said, "Stop!" and the woman stopped in puzzlement. Then the ex-queen turned to the dreamer and said, "See!"

Then the ex-queen said, "Not enough?" Then she told the young woman to kill him. The woman got up from the ground. The ex-queen handed her a knife. She went up to the dreamer and stabbed him. To the amazement of the ex-queen, he did not resist her. Finally, he fell dead.

The ex-queen was rejoicing and all that was with her. She then exclaimed that she was the new dreamer. She was getting ready to kill the young woman that did her bidding. The young woman was pleading for her life. However, during this action, the dream turned dark and violent. Objects were moved out of place from the agitation generated within the dream.

Unexpected by the ex-queen, the dreamer resurrected himself within the dream. Then the ex-queen observed the inflicted stab wound disappeared. The young woman was scared, weeping, and apologized to the dreamer. She asked, "Can you forgive me?!" He said, "I forgive you." Then the new young woman cried even more. However, the ex-queen was infuriated with his response.

The ex-queen said, "I suppose you are going to forgive me too." He said, "No." She retorts, "She was the one that killed you." His response was, "Yes, she did. It was done under your spell and direction." He pulled the young woman up off the ground and was beginning to clean her up.

The ex-queen grabbed the young woman and said to the dreamer, "Look, I am still in control over her." As she was dragging her away from the dreamer, the dreamer said to the ex-queen, "Look behind you." The ex-queen looked. The woman that she had grabbed with her hand was still standing before the dreamer.

The ex-queen said to the dreamer, "Did you just created another young woman?" He said, "No. This is the same one that killed me." She said, "Then who is this young woman?" His reply, "You have the same woman. The one you have wanted to kill me. The one I have was forced to kill me. After all this is my dream, and I can do whatsoever I want. I chose to divide the nature of the young woman and make this one whole once again."

The ex-queen turned to walk away with the young woman wondering whether to kill her in front of the dreamer. He then commanded the ex-queen to stop. She was going to laugh at him, but she could not move! He took the crown that was on her head off her and gave it to the new woman. He said to the ex-queen, "You knew my love in marriage, she did not. You have tormented me and her. Now, it's your turn to be tormented." The ground opened from under the ex-queen. She fell into a fiery pit with the one she had in her hand, all her lovers and those with her. Then the ground closed upon them.

Courting her as he had once planned, the love relationship returned to both. Then there was another wedding. They were as happy as before all the chaos occurred. It was as if the ex- queen never existed. This time the dream will last forever with everyone aware of the dream and in the same level of happiness before they became aware of it.

Devorah-7C2 reappeared on the screen and said, "From that, you can see why repentance is so important. At any rate, that is our simile of the purpose of the formulation of this universe. This universe never was intended to be the final resting place for existence. According to the faint star-writings, there was a war in the previous universe. The favorite creature of that universe waged war against the creator. About one third of the creatures were defeated, arrested, and set aside for final punishment. Then the creation of this universe was set up to create the replacement set of those banished. The adversary of human beings seduced and continues to seduce humans into submission to do his bidding. When he enticed Adam and Eve to eat the forbidden fruit, he thought he had won.

Afterward, he saw that there was another plan. He tried to destroy the salvation plan for humans by genetically altering the human race until there was nearly no natural human left, hence the flood. Once again, he tried to get mankind condemned at the Tower of Babel. Next was at the crucifixion of Yeshua (Jesus). Each time he thought he won. The next plan is the creation of the great apostasy of the believers, in which, he will come to rule the earth. However, this time he knows he has been defeated. We showed the primary plot, but there were many plots. After this universe is over, those found worthy will replace those evil beings.

Epilogue...

Mankind does not truly learn from history. That is why history always repeats itself. Each generation must overcome their individualized challenges. While each challenge is painted differently, the nature of the challenge is always the same. In some cases, it is overcoming drugs, in others it could be overcoming bitterness, yet others it may be some form of oppression.

Within each, there is a need for the implication of some obvious rational answer. Emotional charged reasoning will always destroy rational reasoning if we let it. Often the emotional response paints its reasoning as a rational recourse of the given situation. In more individual terms, each of us must overcome our individual sin nature.

Lastly, all history is written in stone: past, present, and future. Our individual choices are already incorporated into the future. Incredible as it may seem, we choose to be on one side of the line or the other. This choice has already been made- not for us but by us. We travel through time proving that it is our choice.

Afterward, Eliyahu-0X0, Devorah-7C2, Katool-0A3 and little &11 appeared together on the screen. Eliyahu-0X0 said that it was important for us to warn the people, of this era of time, about their pending judgment. It is about to fall upon all the people of this time for their recent rebellion against the creator.

Devorah-7C2 then spoke. She told us that they knew that this would be their last interaction with us. She thought it was funny that this recording was made before they met us. She wished us the best and said goodbye. Then all the androids said goodbye. It was a very emotional moment for all of us because we knew that we would never see them again in this lifetime.

Considering our task, we had to come up with some kind of strategy to accomplish our mission. Obviously, we were going to be writing this book. We have all the data that we needed from our journeys. However, to create change in the present day was an ominous task.

Margo spoke up, this information will not truly generate any change. I was puzzled at first. I asked her, "What do you mean?" She said that just knowing information will only change opinions and behaviors temporarily. People truly need to learn from history. However, they can't. This is not entirely their fault. They need a conversion of their soul. Otherwise, when information is emotionally charged, all rational logic becomes abandoned. They say and do things that they normally would not do. The human soul is weak. There is only one way to convert the soul.

Converting the soul means that the soul needs a connection with the Holy Spirit. There are many spirits in the world. Connect with them, they will pull you to their path of destruction. Only the Holy Spirit will show the way to safety. To achieve this, there is a need to repent of the sins committed to the true God. Then there is an absolute need to believe that Yeshua (Jesus in English) died for those sins. The next step is to make Yeshua the Lord over your actions. Tell others of your choice. Finally, there is a need to join in fellowship with other believers. This will aid in keeping yourself sensitive to the Spirit.

Trying to change the outcome of the world was no longer our objective. Changing the minds of people within the time that we live in cannot be assured. All we can do is change some of the individuals we meet. When enough people make the conversion; at times, this is enough to change the tide of a nation. This is our hope.

The End